AN APPLE IN HER HAND

A COLLECTION FROM THE HUDSON VALLEY WOMEN'S WRITING GROUP

COLLEEN GERAGHTY

KIT GOLDPAUGH

EILEEN HOWARD

TANA MILLER

MARY K O'MELVENY

JAN ZLOTNIK SCHMIDT

KAPPA WAUGH

CODHILL
PRESS

2018

CODHILL
PRESS

Codhill books are published by
David Appelbaum for Codhill Press

AN APPLE IN HER HAND: A COLLECTION FROM THE HUDSON VALLEY WOMEN'S WRITING GROUP

Book Design by Jana Potashnik
BAIRDesign, Inc. · bairdesign.com

ISBN 978-1-949933-00-0
Printed in the United States of America

CONTENTS

INTRODUCTION

> **"Another belief of mine: that everyone else my age is an adult, while I am merely in disguise."**
>
> **-MARGARET ATWOOD**

In our youth-oriented culture, the wisdom, joy, determination, moral compass, and sheer talent of older women creative writers are too often neglected or ignored. The authors of this collection, **An Apple in Her Hand,** are seven older women from diverse backgrounds who are members of a longstanding Hudson Valley writing group, which is dedicated to personal artistic growth as well as celebrating community. The cohesive group is composed of academics, a social worker, a psychiatric nurse, a teacher, and a lawyer. Some are retired, some are still working, some are musicians. All are volunteers, activists and artists.

The various sections of the book --- Remembrance, Joy, Visibility, Resistance, Resilience, Transformation, Aging, and Bearing Witness --- grew from the authors' individual passions and from their collective perspective of being women-of-a-certain-age in a culture that tends to render older women invisible, irrelevant. This collection dispels that erroneous perception by addressing these universal themes in a compelling manner that can engage readers of all ages and backgrounds.

These writings, memoir, poetry, and prose, are different from one another in many ways. After a reading given by the group, a woman asked, "How can you work together as writers when your work is so different?" The answer is simple. As a group, the members respect literature in all its forms. They do not adhere to a one-and-only-one way to create point of view. Instead, they believe in the power of difference to transform both literature and life.

An Apple in Her Hand is a book crafted from myriad bits and pieces, often beautiful, often profound, often humorous. These works come together with strength, honesty, and power. The disparate perspectives of these authors, as well as their artistry, both demand and deserve to be seen and heard.

The book's title, *An Apple in Her Hand*, and the poems in the first chapter of this anthology, were inspired by a sculpture of Colleen Geraghty's entitled "Ciotóg."

Colleen Geraghty
Ciotóg

Once upon a time
girl
moaning on the shore
girl
dark moon rising
girl
slippery-tongued, stroppy
girl
wild-eyed, bitchy
girl
drink the pitch tar
girl
eat the damn crow
girl
drink the white cream
girl
bury yourself in blood
girl
cut out your own tongue
girl
bolt the goddamn door
girl
brilliant black-eyed, blue
girl
bury yourself alive
girl
silent, secret, strange
girl
scaly, scabby, filthy
girl
fat girl, glutton girl
ugly, stupid bitch
girl
slut girl, whore girl.

›

dirty piece of fur
girl
tramp girl, gulp girl
choke girl
choke girl
swallow heaven's sludge
girl
ocean, moon, and star
girl
bone and grizzle and broth
girl
ride the wave dark
girl
hide behind the moon
girl
cremate your own knowing
girl
bury the torch deep
girl
stoke the sullied cauldron
girl
brilliant hot char
girl
sacrifice the nice
girl

Born again in light
girl
Born again in night
girl

*Ciotóg – Irish word for left-handed –
One who does not sit on the right hand
side of God.

Eileen Howard

Apples or Oranges

In the appellate apple court
Eve is holding her own.
Beleaguered and heckled
she stands all alone.

"Ad astra per ardua"
I reached for the stars.
Can I help if my eye
was caught by an apple?

I was tired of no clothes,
craved ribbons and furbelows.
Thought an apple red cape
would slake my desires.

I bit off scraps of peel
Just for my wish book:
licked my fingers and oh....
'twas crisp and delicious.

I nibbled some more...
The Gardener was furious!
I treasure the garden.
Your reasoning is spurious.

I fling myself on your mercy.
I repent. I'm so sorry.
I ask the court for forbearance.
Forever? Don't ban us!

Her brow furrowed,
a cloud crossed her visage.
Then she straightened and
dimpled.

No, I'm not sorry.
We were created coequals.
I'm opting for free will...
Throw in some stilettos!

Kappa Waugh

What I Hold

The words of my mouth
are not curses or incantations
not accusations but rather names
from the orchard garden
gala braeburn pippin jonagold

The bracelets on my wrists
are not precious metals. No gold
or silver, but curling appleskins
rubyred yellowgreen
speckled spotted streaked.

The food on my plate
is not prey no slaughtered victim
of my appetites but compote
tart applesauce chutney
baked apple in a pastry crust.

The object that I grasp
is not a sword whip or grenade
no calculator no bill of sale
I hold a round tafaha aeble
jabuka an apple in my hand.

Jan Zlotnik Schmidt

One Succulent Bite

Red gloss a sheen
that promises dreaming

One bite one crunch
into the flesh of the fruit

Sweet and tart down the gullet
one succulent taste

Then she stretches her arms upward
almost touching cloud and sky

She could embrace
the bole of an ash

Send leaves fluttering
with her breath

Send them floating
into a world

that will not dispel her words
or deny her power.

Tana Miller

The Apple Was a Pomegranate

deep within the fertile garden
grew the Tree of Knowledge
guarded by swarms of hummingbirds
suckled by perpetual summer

God's own pomegranates
hung from the tree's branches
gravid with fleshy seed   red juice

edgy   questing Eve was sorely tempted

this fruit is forbidden God roared
when he saw Eve's yearning

Eve had to know
            to decide for herself
one day   hands shaking   heart determined
she plucked a burnished pomegranate from the tree
pressed it to her lips   sucked deep
passed it to Adam's waiting mouth

the creatures in Paradise screamed   the sun blinked
God beat deep lament upon his chest

humankind turned on its heel

Kit Goldpaugh

The Kitchen Witch

Beneath the earth
a seed sinks and splits
roots shoot out like spider webs

A swaddled sapling stands protected
      through snow and summer
        its blossoms burst with promises of pies and tarts,
   of evidence to Eve's weak will and Paris's poor choice,
  of witch weaponry
      or ammunition against Dorothy and the tin man

A basket of apples sits on the table:
pies
   tarts
  turnovers

The child places a Golden Delicious
  in her grandmother's hand

The grandmother pushes pins in its flesh
  two eyes, a nose, a mouth
     sits it on the windowsill

Long after the pies are eaten,
it shrinks and withers, waiting in the window

On a white winter night
the old woman and child gather scraps of
calico, bits of gingham, a ribbon, buttons, threads, twine
They stitch and stuff and snip
  Now the apple has a face, a body
  a dress, a pointed black hat and shoes, hair
  a broom
Suspended in the window
she protects the kitchen the child the old woman.

Mary K O'Melveny

An Apple in Her Hand

Eve was our very first
object lesson.
I have always imagined
that leering snake sated
with laughter at how easy
it was to spoil everything,
his forked tongue a fulsome
symbol of desire gone wrong,
pain filling in the blanks.
Think of how she had to slink
away from paradise,
naked and bewildered,
all for the sake of one
taste of some carnelian
sheathed fruit. As she hurried
away from light's visible
spectrum toward a world
filled with violence and danger,
she was still spitting out seeds,
her tongue consumed by flames.

EMEMBERANCE

Kappa Waugh

Tidewater, VA, 1949

Those were the names:
Billy, Tooter, Becky Lou, Buddy,
children we played with then.
We all lived on Sorority block
in that dusty southern town.

This was food we ate:
cressie, burgoo, spoonbread, pork roll;
snacks were Moon pies, dog biscuits,
bread & sugar. We ate non-foods too:
pencil erasers, boogers, paper sucker sticks.

This was what we wore:
for boys, shorts, long pants, bib overalls;
girls wore dresses. Girls' underwear—
white cotton or pastel days-of-the-week,
Y-fronts or nothing for the boys.

This was what we believed:
bitten fingernails went to your appendix.
Crossed eyes could stick that way, and
step on a crack, break your mother's back.
God could see you even in the bathroom.

This was what happened: all gone.
Billy dead at six under a car. Tooter,
a survivalist, walked into the woods, but
never out. Becky Lou felled by childbirth.
Buddy ate his daddy's gun.

Jan Zlotnik Schmidt
Fade Out/Fade In

A little boy's face, a child's lips, curly brown hair, a cap and knickers. He sits on a Shetland pony, fading patches of white on the horse's rump. I don't know whether he's living in the apartment on Atlantic Avenue near Pinchuk Paints or the house on Fort Hamilton Parkway. Once he told me that his mother put him on the trolley in front of the paint store, and he traveled alone to first grade. Down Flatbush almost to the river—the electric lines of the streetcar sparking in the sun. He never said if he was afraid or happy to be on an adventure. He never told me much more about his childhood.

I look at him—back stiff, eyes turned to an invisible observer. Why did these Russian immigrant parents take this picture? The father knew no English except the words he needed for business and signed his name with an X; the mother made borsch, shav and boiled chicken. Was it their hope that their boy would be a Tom Mix, a real American cowboy? With a half-smile or half-grimace (it is hard to tell), he sits quietly, patiently, waiting. Anticipating his future in a new world. And always there was his silence.

But it's his eyes that let me know who he was: small, dark, piercing. Sad. These same eyes are mine. I am three, sitting on a stool, half facing an easel, paint brush in my hand, ready to dot the empty canvas with color. Half turned to the camera, I hear my parents' commands—smile—smile—but I don't want to. I wonder why they have me dressed in a flowered smock, ready to be an artist. Why are adults so foolish? I don't want to be the subject of the camera's eye. But I say nothing.

Now his lips are sealed—his eyes almost dissolving into his skull. He glances at me—not a flicker of recognition. Gingerly he picks up smashed pieces of white bread between his fingers, brings them to his mouth, slowly chews. I watch; I wonder. Words close up inside me too—and they burn my throat.

When I ask my younger sister about the photograph, she tells me it wasn't my father—it was his brother, our uncle Mike. She's not sure though. Not sure at all.

Tana Miller

Where the Big Bass Bite

the tearing from the warm bed before dawn
the ride to the lake stretched across the lumpy back seat
the vibration of the engine   tires   becoming my universe
when the car stops   I breathe the delicious fish/dead plant smell
as I bail water from the bottom of the boat
slip the oars into the locks   row into the fog
silently skirt the shore where tree branches
hang low above deep holes
I dip each oar quietly into the dark water
I know we can't let the bass hear us
he signals to stop   chooses a lure   casts   waits
waits   reels in the line   casts again
we never speak a word
the sun rises slowly   the sky lightens to gray
transforms to pale blue
the air warms
a bite   he finesses the fish
pulls it flopping gasping open-mouthed into the boat
I study the fish's wide eyes as he pulls the hook from its lips
throws it thrashing on the bottom of the boat
I watch it go slack
the sun is hot now   I tug at the thick orange life vest I wear
my empty stomach rumbles
early swimmers make splashes across the lake
I wish I knew how to swim
I trail my hand in the cool water   dream of standing up
jumping over the side of the boat
what could he do?
an oar slips from my grasp with a sudden splash
he swears at me   reels his empty line in fast
his mouth hard   his eyes flat black stones
that's it he says   you stay home from now on

my heart as cold as the dead fish's eyes
I whip the boat around
row hard toward the dock

Mary K O'Melveny

The Mathematics of Parking

I am parking the car.
I am quite excellent at this.
People comment often
on my ability to slide in,
a quick wheel turn or two,
it's done. I walk away.

My father taught me to park.
A lesson in pure geometry.
Mathematics determined
most of his daily moves.
Like making all the beds
with precise hospital corners.

The beauty of calculus,
or so he would say,
was in having the right answers.
Mistakes were never
acceptable. Careful
proofs produced satisfaction.

Perhaps his great anger
grew from our quite human limitations.
Pen to paper, word to ear
not always a numeric certainty.
Instead, we struggled to relate.
Formulas elusive, answers clouded.

Home from the Great War
(how innocent everyone was back then),
he had already lost interest
in succession. Wanted out.
But instead he got three kids.
Six heart attacks. Algorithmic bad luck.

We never liked each other much.
My mother cried too often.
I computed the statistical relationship

between his presence or absence
and the sadness that filled our rooms.
It was significant.

I remember driving with her
over dark mountain roads
to the VA Hospital ER.
Siblings boarded with neighbors.
I could never tell if the substance
filling up the car was fear or relief.

But somehow he beat the odds.
Again. Like a savvy gambler
shaving with a plastic razor
in the casino bathroom,
smiling into the mirror, red–rimmed
eyes smarting from morning light.

Later on, the numbers did run out.
Someone retrieved me from
my college English class
(so much more warm and fluid
than arithmetic computations),
to deliver the somber news.

I am older now than he was then.
I have lists of questions
I never asked him. Not to mention
answers I think might be correct.
But who can ever know?
Our universes did not compute.

So I wonder what we might have said
to each other now, taking careful
measure like long-dead stars
realigning briefly to see if logic mattered.
I know I would surely say,
Thanks for the parking lessons.

Colleen Geraghty

My Real Mother

My real mother didn't believe in no God, Jesus, or the Holy Ghost. She believed in cotton candy and peppermints, soft pink dresses, nylon stockings, and high heels. She believed in Chesterfields and two-piece bathing suits and the Philadelphia trolley. My real mother turned her back on the tight-lipped, back-biting, holier-than-thou bitches from the Rosary Society and lived a different life where she called the shots.

My real mother wasn't no spring garden waiting to be plowed. She was a silk slipped, baby-oiled-and-iodine suntanned beauty who rode the trolley to Center City to buy her and me some new yellow sundresses and a couple of pretty little pocketbooks. She didn't board that iron snake like the rest of them Catholic ladies who were fat as cows and on their way to see the baby doctor, their bellies so swollen they could barely walk, let alone see their feet. Their brats screaming while their big kids tight-fisted the wrists of their littler kids or slapped them around to keep them in line, the whole wailing brood stinkin' like shit and piss and sour spit-up.

My real mom wasn't nothing like them lumbering, fat, blue-veined bitches who could barely make it up two steps into the trolley. My real mom was long-legged and delicate as a bird, the small wings in her back poking through a blush of peach silk, the skirt of her dress swooshing in the hot summer air as she tip-toed up into that trolley.

My real mom wasn't bound for no baby doctor. She wasn't plopping down on the sweaty seat with a belly so big she couldn't see her ugly pregnant feet. She wasn't hoisting fidgeting babies on each hip, wielding a diaper, wiping teething biscuit goo and sour milk off no cranky snot-faced babies while the rest of her brats whined, "I'm hot...I gotta pee...Are we there yet?"

My real mom was sitting pretty, her small, beaded pocketbook open in her lap, her soft hand opening a compact, powdering her nose, smoothing pink lipstick around her pretty lips. My real mom was kissing a tissue and smiling at me, taking out an elegant little oriental fan that she'd gotten from some Chink lady down on the avenue, flicking it open and waving it back and forth to keep us cool. My real mom didn't stink like no diaper pail but smelled fresh and easy as a summer morning. The two of us would sit there on that trolley like a miracle while all them other moms were hollering and sweatin' like pigs.

My real mom only had one kid to bother about and that kid was me. Without a big brood to take care of and no baby in her belly, she didn't spend her time kneeling, sitting, standing, and praying to Good-God-Almighty that she'd survive pushing another brat outa her bloody hole. Instead of wiping snot and tears, piss and shit off a bunch of brats on a trolley bound for the baby doctor, my mom was taking us shopping at John Wannamaker's. She was opening her little beaded bag and offering me a peppermint.

We sat on that trolley in our peppermint bubble, her little beaded purse on her lap sparkling like a pile of jewels, her long sleek legs crossed at the ankles while she fanned us Oriental-style. Every once in a while, she'd whisper silky words into my ear where they fell like cherry blossoms, and I'd smile and lean into her, so happy. I'd look across the aisle at them fat-ass pregnant rosary cows and wonder how jealous they were that my real mom didn't believe in their Holy Goddamn make-a-baby-for-Jesus-every-year God.

I'd watch them bitches watching my real mom and me as we rocked along in that heavy iron trolley, and sometimes I'd fall asleep with the rhythm and bliss of having her all to myself! I was always shocked, every time, when the trolley screeched to a stop and I woke up, and my real mother, the one with the Oriental fan, she was gone.

And me? I was still in that trolley, sitting next to some fat Rosary Society cow, posing as my real mother, and we were up to our eyeballs in shit and piss, sour-milk, and a bunch of goddamn shrieking babies who Father Finnegan said were nothing but blessings from God, gifts from heaven.

Jan Zlotnik Schmidt

Leopard Housecoat

During her last days my mother
shuffled from bed to bath
to kitchen table,
her feet scraping against
the cracked linoleum.

Step on a crack
Break your mother's back
Step on a line
Break your father's spine

A child, I stepped carefully over
the ruts and spider lines
in pavement, assured
my parents would live forever.
I would make it so.

In the evening she played
Scrabble on the kitchen table,
making nonsense words
nonsense syllables
as she straightened the round collar
of her leopard housecoat.

We played into the night.
She cuffed each sleeve, smoothed the creases,
cupped her hands in her lap
as she pondered the board.

We didn't correct her.
Then her words:
"Quiet.
The leopards are sleeping."

Kit Goldpaugh

Things My Mother Taught Me

That

when a sales clerk suggests
less expensive jewelry, shoes, handbags
remember
the clerk in the pretty pearls
and black knit dress earns
minimum wage
(her condescension a job requirement)

that

you should never arrive anywhere swinging
your arms
(better to cancel than to show up
empty handed)

that

company table is set from the outside in
the cutlery staged sequentially
from soup spoon to dessert fork
(knives turned in)

that

you can judge a man's worth by
the care and devotion he gives his mother
(and that
virginity matters to him and sex hurts for you)

that

what goes on in this house stays in this house
(like
the secret smell of ether from the pharmacist
that makes the kittens sleep deeply
in a blanket
in a box
on their open windowed car ride
to a farm in Saugerties)

that

the shoebox marked *mission medicine*
held vaccines and vitamins for African babies
(not Aunt Claire's private duty surplus reserve
of Darvon and valium).

that

if a bird flies into your house
soon someone you know will die
and

that

if you are bad to your mother in life, her hand
will rise in death
from the grave
every night
(and you will have to inter it anew every day)

and that

it's a sin to make fun of people
(because her father had a very bad limp and
she had a cast in her eye)
(which I always found beautiful until
she told me otherwise).

Kappa Waugh

My First Pet

My First Pet

The porch floor is gritty under my knees. Where my brother kneels next to me, I am sweating. We're watching our guinea pigs mate. David, white with a smutty nose, rumbles and weaves his hips as he crowds red-eyed Martha. She chews on a carrot.

David mounts her, clasping her furry sides with his tiny paws. My parents stand behind us watching. My mom says, "Now they'll know about S-E-X." Martha keeps eating, but has moved on to a lettuce leaf. David climbs off and starts chewing the carrot. My dad asks us, "What do you think about that?" I ask him, "Do youall eat during S-E-X?"

My First Job

You could see the old man's feet hurt. He shuffled slowly around the ring, leading the fat pony while its little rider kicked and kicked the pony's sides, crying, "Giddyup!" I, a horse-mad nine year old, bargained with the man. I'd lead the riders around the ring if I could ride when times were slack. "Come at ten on Sattiday," he said. By five o'clock Saturday, my inappropriate sandals had raised multiple blisters, my hair fell lank with sweat and dust around my grimy face, and my teeth grated with pony-ring dirt. I had walked over nine miles, for a total of three rides around the ring. The old man asked, "Coming back next Sattiday?"

My Best Christmas Present Ever

We'd opened our stockings, run the obligatory slinky race down the back stairs, and tried to hide the evidence of silly putty stuck to the rug. We'd choked down our Christmas oatmeal while waiting for our parents to finish their eggnog. Time for presents! Mine was an 18 inch tall, plaster Joan of Arc, dressed in armor, wearing a sword. The French fleur-de-lis flag furled part way around her. She gazed toward heaven as I gazed at her with undying devotion. For the next six months she lay next to me each night, hearing my prayers, watching over me as I slept crowded against the wall so she could have all the pillow space. But one night my brothers invaded my room for a tickle attack; my thrashing about knocked Joan off the bed and destroyed her as thoroughly as her martyrdom at the stake five hundred years before.

My First Hangover

Oh, yes, I knew how precious I looked as a five-year-old flower girl at my aunt's wedding. I smirked and preened, kissed the handfuls of rose petals before tossing them in the aisle. The church smelled of beeswax, incense and the perfume of cooing, teary-eyed women. After the ceremony came the photographs, the champagne toasts, the cake. While the grownups slow-danced, I drifted around drinking up each half-finished champagne glass. When I got dizzy, I snuck under the head table. Later I threw up in my aunt's kicked-off satin pumps.

My First Chainsaw

You might ask why a pre-pubescent child was given a chainsaw in the first place. And you would be right. Some stories are just better left untold.

Kappa Waugh

Four, Five, Six, Seven

I am four.
Morning stars are singing
as my mother whips me.
My cowboy belt strikes
across the air, churning
dust motes through the light.
To my surprise, God alights
to stand with me; neither
of us cries. In my house
courage is admired.

I am five.
Exiled to my grandparents
because my mother's crazy,
or I'm bad. Who cares?
I've learned to read, and the world
flops open, a loose-limbed book
of wonder. Giotto in *Life Magazine*
paints a black devil lurking while
the hand of God pierces the sky.
Anguished angels at the Crucifixion
show me how to grieve.

I am six.
Riding through the dark night to
front seat murmurs from my mother
and her lover. I crank the window down
shout hymns at the winter air.
When my snot runs too fast for singing,
I pull back in, shut out the wind.
Huffed breath mists the glass so my
trigger finger can draw hearts:
KSA plus G for God.

I am seven.
In the convent school I've told
Sister Claire my family's
Holy Catholic, not Roman,
and Sister has explained to the
whole third grade that all my family
will burn in hell forever.
And ever. After an eternity of terror
and regret I hear the sigh
of God, who knows better.

Jan Zlotnik Schmidt

I Met My Mother's Body at Loehmann's

"Loehmann's Closing Down After 94 Years"
(*New York Times,* January 24, 2014)

I met my mother's body for the first time at Loehmann's. There she was in a girdle, with those tabs for beige stockings, a white bra and half-slip, staring down at me, a child looking up into the expanse of her flesh, her curves, her midriff bulging over her slip's elastic band. I was six or seven or eight years old, crouching down, peering up at a glade of women's legs—some stalk thin, some stockinged, some pudgy at the calves. And gazing upward there were the serviceable Playtex bras, a glimpse of them, as they tried on blouses, sweaters, and jackets. We were at the back of the store—there were no dressing rooms—and in front of me were the gilt circular staircase, the crystal chandelier, enormous diamonds of filigreed glass, refracting the little afternoon light in the room. At the entrance, the men sat and waited, hunched over their *Times,* or *Herald Tribune,* or *New York Mirror,* women's pocketbooks dangling from their arms, eyes looking down, not daring that taboo glance to the back of the store.

The women became Circe, Dido, the Graces, preening in front of the mirror in cashmere or silk, or sleek black shirts, asking for approval first from the women and then from the men. They had beehive dyed blonde and brown hair, perfectly manicured white or pink nails, straight lines in their hose, and a hint of Arpege perfumed the air. After gazing

with satisfaction at their profiles in the mirror, they praised each other for their keen eyes and instinct for the bargain, the cashmere coat originally 59.00 down to 29.00, the B. Altman's blouse a steal for 6.95 down from 9.95. Their bodies, ready, girded for battle with a larger world, a world in which they wouldn't be viewed as immigrants or imposters. They had the right clothes. And I, patient, sat cross-legged, staring into my future.

Loehmann's remained a constant in my relationship with my mother—each time I returned home from college, from adult life teaching in Kentucky, from middle age boredom, my mother and I would go to the new stores, first on Flatbush Avenue and Duryea Place and then to Sheepshead Bay. At that point we knew each other's mode of being. I went for the turtlenecks and black pants, she for silk blouses and rayon stretch pants. And she always made me try on a bigger size. The tunic revealed too much of my breasts, or the shirt, she said, popped open at the buttons, or the blazer pulled across my back. My mother, jealous of my lithe body, hers so stocky and stout, unconsciously pulled me into her world by convincing me to go for the larger size—the sweaters wouldn't fit under the coat, she would say, or you don't want to reveal every bulge of flesh. But I wanted the knit tops that emphasized my figure or the blazer that created curves. Then we'd argue until I gave in, unsure of my desirability.

There also were the conversations that passed for intimacy in the dressing room or in the elevator between the racks of sportswear on the first floor and the second floor Back Room, Designer Showroom. "How are you doing?" she'd ask in a crowded elevator as the other women listened. And what could I say? "Oh fine." She once questioned me in a particularly difficult period in my marriage, and I realized that the advice about clothing would have to pass for closeness. She really didn't want to enter my inner world. The intimacy of the dressing room would have to be enough.

Later in her old age, I was the one pressing the creases of clothes in place, straightening out the crepe blouses, pulling up the rayon pants because she couldn't bend down because of her arthritis. I was the one who helped her pull the cotton sweaters over her head, I was the one who heard her worries about dying as she tried on Kelly green silk blouses, and I was the one who saw the empty left sac of her cotton bra. We still had Loehmann's—the ritual of dressing ourselves, the ritual of advice, the ritual of caring.

Five years after my mother's death, I am in a Loehmann's in Boca Raton, Florida. The communal dressing room is empty. I try on a salmon pink silk shirt with pearl buttons. A shade that says look at me. I slowly close the buttons, swallowing hard, remembering too much of my past, looking around the dressing room for someone to ask for advice. Now I have

some of my mother's body—a slight paunch of a belly, thick upper arms. But I still am tall and fairly thin. I sashay this way and that, gazing at myself in the full length mirror, not sure of the blaring color. A young Russian girl, a Lolita-lookalike, comes in; she tries on a yellow bikini and a black net beach cover-up. I gaze at myself in the mirror. "That looks nice."

"Really?"

"Yes. It's a good color for you. With the hair."

I smooth down my silver hair.

"Buy it. The color is just right for you."

Suddenly I miss my mother.

JOY

Kit Goldpaugh

Candlemas Day

Before my brother Wendell gave me a Punxsutawney Phil groundhog cookie cutter, I had to make my groundhog cookies from a squirrel mold. Before baking, I amputated the squirrels' tails and reshaped their little asses. The Phil cutter makes things much more efficient.

I've celebrated Groundhog Day for as far back as I can remember. I recall in elementary school, thinking myself hilarious, asking students and teachers alike if they had seen their shadows. In college, drunk, I called my sister and her new husband the accountant, cross country-collect- to inquire about their shadow hunting. I reversed the charges because

1. I only had a quarter left

2. It was Ladies' Night at the Black Cat in Oneonta

3. It was February 2

My sister was alarmed and mortified and asked, not rhetorically, if I thought I was funny. Obviously, I thought I was funny. That was the reason for the call. That and the Ladies' Night cheap beers.

February 2 falls midway between the Winter Solstice and Spring Equinox. For thousands of years, star watchers have noted this point in the earth's rotation. It is one of the four celestial crosses that fall between the solstices and equinoxes, Imbolc on Feb 2 and Beltane on May 1, along with Samhain

and Lughnasadh which fall during mid-summer and autumn. Even before the Druids' celebrations, this celestial point was acknowledged in ancient stories. One Imbolc story tells of an old woman who gathers all the wood she can find and sets it ablaze on Feb.2. The firelight is so great that it pushes winter away. An animal would cast a great shadow in that light. If there is no fire, there is no shadow, and a long winter will continue because the old woman slept through the day of opportunity. The stories change, but given the prehistoric absence of satellites and meteorologists, a long shadow from a rodent in February was as accurate a predictor of spring as any other measure.

If there was an ancient pagan ceremony, there will be a corresponding Christian one usurping it, usually with a misogynistic twist. Imbolc is no exception. About six weeks after Christmas, the church celebrates a three-fold holy day on Candlemas Day, February 2. It marks the first time that Jesus enters the temple as well as his formal Presentation in said temple. It is also the Blessed Virgin Mother's purification (same temple), kind of a six-week OB-GYN check-up, for the holiest and purest of women. As a reminder, Feb. 2 became the day that the church would purify all its candles for the upcoming year.

In Catholic school in the early 60's, children marched to church every Feb.3

to have their throats blessed with those newly empowered candles in honor of St. Blaise who either warded off wild animals with crossed combs, or, while in prison, cured a boy from choking on a fish bone by either touching him with candles on his throat or laying his hands on the boy's head or throat. Reports vary. He became the patron saint of wool makers, weavers and ENT doctors alike. Although St. Blaise Day is not directly connected to Groundhog Day, it does demonstrate how far the old Christian men would go to claim a day. Also, this is useful information in a round of Groundhog Fact or Crap. The saint who is honored on Feb.2 is actually St. Joan de Lestonnac, a nun who formed an order to care for plague victims, but what fun is that?

As a middle school teacher, I was required to understand seasonal changes and reflect them in my bulletin boards, a monthly task as much fun as purchasing tampons. February meant groundhogs, dead presidents, valentines, snow closings and delays and Ash Wednesday. It also meant that there was a faculty or departmental meeting, or professional development session rescheduled every afternoon to compensate for the endless cancellations in this short month. I covered the bulletin board with red hearts and a calendar of cancellations. It was a pitiful display of forced cheer.

Eliot was wrong. April is not the cruelest month. That title belongs to February, which is cruel, cold, and lonely, especially if one does not have a Valentine. Not everyone has a sweetheart, but everyone can love a rodent. I started thinking about these things in January, as soon as school was back in session from Winter Break, formerly known as Christmas Break. Everyone would need a mid-winter break. And so it began. During one dark and dreary faculty meeting when I'd grown tired of playing Naked Action Faculty Figures, I wrote the first invitation. On the cover, I scribbled,

The Shadow and the Groundhog,
melody = The Holly and the Ivy

The shadow and the groundhog
And the chucking of the wood
Of all the days of wintertime
Groundhog day is the good
est
When you haven't had a snow day
And you think you just might die
That's the time to have a toast
And get a little high

The next step was to set a time and date and print out the invitations. Party planning warded off the winter blues. The decorations were simple but time consuming. I traced and cut little felt groundhogs, gave them googly eyes and suspended them from the chandelier with dental floss. Plastic top hats were on sale after New Year's Eve, so I stocked up on hats. Hats and scarfs for photo ops. One year at Christmas, my brother gave me a groundhog puppet, and Lil' Phil joined the reenactment of the official shadow search in Punxsutawney from that year on. Wendell fully supported the annual party with gifts of the heart: the cookie cutter, the puppet, the mug, and one year he outdid himself by writing a songbook.

Themed parties need games. This

party's games included Groundhog Fact or Crap and Pin the Shadow on the Groundhog. Fact or Crap was set up in the center of the table. Two hats and a toilet were labeled Choose, Fact, Crap. Historical and astrological fun facts were mixed in with nonsense in a plastic top hat labeled **_Choose._** Strips of paper might say, "In the paleolithic era, groundhogs laid eggs." That one would end up in the **_Crap_** toilet shaped mug. A strip reading "The tradition of Groundhog Day that we celebrate today has ancient celestial origins." That strip would go in the mortar board graduation cap labeled **_Fact._** Guests often invented new pieces of information for the sorting hat, such as, "Genetically, just behind the chimpanzee, the groundhog is most closely related animal to the homo-sapien, having a 93% DNA match" or "Millenia before the Bill Murray movie, the ancient Tibetan monks revered the Lhasa- hedgehog as a symbol of reincarnation." Both are crap, pure crap.

When guests had asked what they could bring, I suggested a drink or dessert, preferably thematic. I made pigs in blankets, chicken pate shaped into a groundhog and garnished with green olive eyes, black olive nose and a big red pepper smile. Guests brought cupcakes with little tootsie roll groundhogs peeking through coconut snow, their little almond sliver teeth just above snow level, and Woodchuck Hard Cider.

What I didn't know the first year but learned quickly is that there are real recipes for all manner of winter and summer rodent. The Louisiana Commission of Game and Wildlife

publishes a booklet just simmering with ideas to serve up the road kill that you might hit, scoop and bag on your ride home. The cook booklet features a nutria, a beagle size rodent like the beast in *The Princess Bride* chasing the young couple through a swamp. Nutria fur coats were popular in the 40's for fashionistas too poor to afford raccoon. The cookbook notes that any large rodent or small mammal – raccoon, squirrel, platypus – can be substituted for nutria. In the cookbook, the headless rodent du jour is dissected into parts like a Da Vinci cartoon. The illustrations help the chef choose which cut of critter to stew, roast or serve up tartare. In the end, everything that this chef prepared tasted like chicken because from the start, that was the plan, chicken with clever names like *rack-o-rodent,* or *woodchuck wonder meat tarts.* I imagined a chicken somewhere looking at a groundhog and contemplating God. It wonders how the wobbling rodent will be honored with a party, at which she will be served up incognito as that filthy animal?!

As I mentioned, nobody got behind a theme like my brother. His "Songs from the Nob" book was a hit. He wrote twenty-four parodies of Christmas carols, and had them printed into a booklet, a hymnal. On the cover was a picture of a group of top hatted and bonneted nineteenth century men and women singing in the candle light of a street lamp while snow falls lightly on their eyelashes and shawls. On the ground beneath the singers and under the same halo of light are a dozen or so groundhogs, also singing and holding their own booklets, *Songs of Imbolc.*

Over the years, I've had to cancel the party, paradoxically, for the very reasons that we needed this party in the first place: Flu. Ice storms. Funerals. That sort of thing. Even the infrequency and irregularity of this annual event seemed to fit the theme. After all, the groundhog is only right about 30% of the time. Like the old woman in the Imbolc legend, I slept through Groundhog Day this year. I did bake a batch of groundhog cookies, though, and left them on my brother's grave for friendly rodents to nibble and bulk up for spring equinox, summer solstice...

Tana Miller

The Barefoot Contessa's Visit*

Ina Garten's in my kitchen at midnight
doesn't she ever sleep?
she's cutting butternut squash in half
chop chop chop

can't this wait? I ask
as I glance askance at the piles
of orange flesh
mounds of seeds   stringy bits
pylons of slippery peel
roly-poly towers of squash
awaiting their turn on tables and counters
like autumn's fancy women lined up for sacrifice
chop chop chop

no time Ina insists
but she puts down her knife
would you like a cocktail? she offers
takes a sizable sip from one of my martini glasses
smacks her lips

no I declare   voice righteous
it is the middle of the night after all
what are you making

well she says   this girl's so much fun
she runs a hand over a squash's sweet curves
she's a butternut slut
I'm making butternut lasagna   ziti   risotto
maybe a soufflé   soup   certainly soup
with apples and coconut curry
butternut ravioli   panzanella   galette
she loves to be boiled broiled roasted braised
baked mashed stewed steamed
what a sport   what a love
chop chop chop

Ina's husband   Jeffrey
curls frosty from the cold air
stomps through my kitchen door
here you are sweetheart he says
places a crate full of squash
on the floor by my stove
who are you? he asks warily
I am aware of my faded flannel nightgown
my calloused bare feet
I   uh   live here I mumble

ah   hello he says
his eyes squint upward   deep
laugh-lines fan out as he smiles
may I fetch you a drink?
I certainly hope you like butternut squash
Ina and Jeffrey laugh and laugh

*Ina Garten was the owner of a popular catering firm, The Barefoot Contessa.
She is currently the host of several cooking shows and the author of many cook
books. Jeffrey is her husband.

Kappa Waugh

Barefoot Burglar

Investigators say "Barefoot Burglar" may have stolen piano.
crawler on CNN News

She stood in the dim room,
her bare toes deep in the Tabriz.
Around her loomed a silent herd
of leather sofas, those urban
bisons of the penthouse set.
"Good hand," she murmured,
fingering the curtains. As for the art,
the frames were better than the oils.
Always a mistake to rely
on the taste of decorators.
But the Steinway made her toes curl.
Ebony sleek, ivory smooth,
harmonious curves and angles.
One phone call and the movers came,
wrapped, hoisted, hauled.
She met the truck in Chelsea.
Only when she was seated,
her foot on the bass pedal
did she realize
she'd left her shoes behind.

Eileen Howard

New York Seder

Middle of the night:
my spinning mind wanders.
Suddenly focuses
on family Seders of old.

My New York relatives
squabble and
bicker.
Talk of shoes and snubs,

trivia and trials.
Children race
through every inch of the house,
are under foot everywhere...

Can you smell the
Matzah ball soup
as it simmers?
Cinnamon of the haroset?

Then the candles are lit.
The table set.
There's a hush and a change.
The children all shush.

Out of slavery into
freedom from trivial pursuits.
Ancient Israelites nod
in silent approbation.

The Haggadah passes round.
Miriam's shade lurks,
concealed in the curtains.
Elijah is quiet.

Out of random chaos
and trite ephemera
suddenly there is
communion:

Ceremonial past
memories.
The bitter herbs
not so bitter.

The four questions
are asked. There are no
squabbles. Solemnity reigns
at the end of the evening.

The afikomen,
the hidden matzah,
is retrieved from my
sleeping daughter:

Next year in Jerusalem
says her smiling Zadih.
The next generation:
hope for us all.

Mary K O'Melveny

Love Nest

As spring's heart flutters toward summer,
I have fallen hopelessly for
two bald eagles who sit on treetops
scanning our reservoir's dinner menu
for their nesting babes. I watch as
they calculate the weight of prey
while the hour darkens. My schoolgirl crush
extends to their nest which fits just so
below the crown of the tallest white pine
that marks the line of our property.
Their cone-shaped aerie looks delicate
but only to visitors stranded on ground.

I am a fool for once unruly branches
now woven and knotted like an heirloom
crazy quilt, innards softened by moss
and grass and cornstalks, embraced
by fallen feathers and stray down.
I am in awe of the way the pair
have built this place together, how
they bonded over each stick and twig,
placed them with purpose like fashionable
decorators. I stare star struck at
each year's remodelings, visual
scrapbooks to each chick who hatched here
then fledged, branched and launched.

I adore how each one warms the egg,
shares the hunt, tears apart the food,
protects the brood, teaches flight.
Most of all, I am mad for their passion –
how they return each season, faithful
and filled with ardor, how they plunge
and swoop, cartwheeling as though
erotica was as new as in
their earliest days, as if they
did not know the perils ahead
or the dangers that winter portends.
As if happy endings were routine.

Woodstock, NY

Kappa Waugh

My Husband Wanted a Swimming Pool Poem

I

Half a million souls swam
through the Tate last year
to see David Hockney's oils.
Azure pools bright in
California sun. No shade,
The heat an iron pressure
in a cloudless sky. Coming
from London's slushy
February streets, wound in
wooly mufflers, tweeds
did the viewers sweat in that
Angelino glare?

II

Piranesi etched antique space,
architectural hulks, vaults,
arches that soar and loom.
Hotel Gellert in Budapest
holds Piranesi baths: pools
salt and sweet, thermal dips,
ice cold plunges. Toute
Budapest lolls there, repairs
their bodies from last week's
trials, girds their loins for
the grueling week to come.

III

Port Ewen's pool requires a
different medium, not oil, not
drypoint. Maybe aquarelle best
paints the pale blue pool, grey
skies above. Those cloudy days
the color comes from bathing
suits, bright candy in a silver
dish. Unlike the London crowd
or the Hungarians, we are not quiet
at all. We splash, shout, drop
cannonballs. Disturb the peace.

Eileen Howard

The Squirrels (and Samantha Cristoforetti) Savor Their Day

From his kitchen in Miami, he feeds
the squirrels using a slingshot made out of
old inner tube and a whittled bit of branch
blown down in some storm

He shoots peanuts at the squirrels through
open glass sliders as he
overlooks his backyard kingdom:
delivers gourmet dining from outer space.
Low tech. Cheap treats.

Above him circles the space station where
an Italian woman now can savor cappuccinos
from a backwards engineered espresso maker
slingshot into orbit from Cape Canaveral
by billionaire Musk.

She grappled it in with a giant robotic arm
engineered and maintained by multiple systems:
smiles in anticipation of a dark roast brew,
reminding her of home and the blue earth below.

Eileen Howard

Nocturnal Turtle

Kisses........
unedited..
A kaleidoscope of
softly melding
kisses.

They flux and shine
brighten...then fade
into another frame of reference:
another world.
They meld and change
yet are all of a piece.

A sigh.

I sidle up and slink a
sly kiss in your ear.
My pink-muscled mollusk
tongue, delves through the
whorls: the
universe
expands.

Lights flow
purple-mauve.
Firework-white-flickers
float through my vision.

Your moans are my
moans.
Or are mine yours?
I don't know.
I don't care.
I just am.
(a kiss).

I am a kiss---
my whole body
throbs kiss rock.
My body rolls kiss-beats
in rock and roll rhythm.

Musing I linger---
tasting your lips----
slurping their sweetness,
lapping their passion:
swimming the tides of
our turbulent togetherness
Coasting on the neap tide---
exploring coral caverns
With roll and caesura
I coast on
our kisses.

My eyes transmuted
periwinkles,
I beach as a
jellyfish:
flotsam on the
tide of
recurrent
passion.
Lost in the current
of passions return.

I beach all jellyfish,
washed out of desire
(which will glow bright again
soon)---an unhurried
blessing.

Right now I'm a jellyfish
beached on the
ocean's feathering-
foam kisses.
Slipping sibilantly
into ocean caverns---
shooshing and foaming
on sand and on seaweed,
with a caesura of volition
with a jellyfish float
as I wash in the tides of our
mutual turn-ons.
The moment of oblivion,
we wash to a standstill---
(in the moment before
we waver and turn...
in the breathless moment
before returning to sea.)

I'm a kiss
I am seaweed
I am coral
I am turtle
and I swim in
the tide as
I float down
your body.
As I waft down your torso
to beach in your
bush.

Where I spelunk
in sweet grottos...
explore secret caverns...
Where I nibble
sea
changed
starfish...
and taste of
anemones...

Where I lap hidden
sea foam,
awash with desire...
and float
freely, freely...
free as a kiss.

Tana Miller

I Hold Your Hand

and feel the tiny rib
bones   once part of a mouse or a mole
a lower jaw bone   a piece of a skull
fragments buried in fur   feathers
deep within the pellet
the barred owl
spit out under the full moon
I feel your fingers
three long-ago broken

I hold your hand love
not a grown up's hand   small
yet battered   crusted
rough from work   neglect
no feminine artifice   no Jelly-Apple or Coral Reef colored nail polish
                    no tamed cuticles
only your wedding ring   a silver circle from Santa Fe

I hold your hand love
as one foot lifts off the earth   I hold your hand love
so I won't fly into space
as my head spins with the planets'
journey around-around-around the sun

I hold your hand love
I hold your hand tight   tighter

VISIBILITY
BREAKING
SILENCE

Mary K O'Melveny

Cease Fire

We are not always happy at the news.
Though one might think we would rejoice.
There is always that uptick in dying
before the eerie silence settles in
like dust filtered on late day's twilight.
Peace tiptoes in on death's long shadows.

Of course the ones who agree are never
those who gather up body parts like dry leaves.
These are the questions no one asked us:
Are we tired of our eardrums breaking apart?
How long must our children sit, dazed and
bleeding, for photographic portraiture?
How will we turn growing piles of bricks and
rubble back into something called a neighborhood?
Did we cry as we left our once green gardens
in search of rubber rafts on open seas?

If there are good answers to these questions,
perhaps peacekeepers are jotting them down
in their computers or cease fire notebooks.
Here is my question for them: Will one of you
be here to walk out with me to the marketplace
just before it starts? In that often forgotten
moment when we place our lives at risk
for a taste of cardamom-spiced coffee.

Tana Miller

The Stations of the Cross: Station 13

Station 13: Jesus' body is taken down from the cross
Setting: Calvary/ Bradley Beach, New Jersey/ 1965

I am with Mary
folded within   her fine blue mantle
my ear pressed against   her shattered heart
as her beloved son is lowered
from the cross   laid across her lap

my arms   intertwined with her arms
help hold her son's long body
his mangled legs dangle
ragged holes ravage both dear hands
his blood soils my skirt
I hold my son   four-months-old
legs still fat   tummy still fat
ice cold oh god so cold
I smooth his wavy hair   study one perfect ear
I am   forever with Mary

Colleen Geraghty

Becoming a Ghost

Was it the night when the whole house buckled under the weight of summer's end, the stifling heat sticking us to our beds, him hammering into the house like a loaded gun, the babies waking when he charged up the stairs, flew into my brother's room, set on him like a hound, his big fists pummeling him awake, was it that night with the babies yowling like startled cats and my little sisters pissing in their beds, my middle sister soaking my leg with hot pee while the street-lights glared into our summer windows, moths batting against the screens, him hammering through the house like a hunting rifle, his rage ricocheting off the rails of the babies' cribs, bunk beds, him throwing my little sisters clear across the room, the other little ones scrambling under their beds, one swift boot in the face, a nose bone crunching, coming loose like a faucet, blood sloshing the floor, a couple of loose teeth, the whole house a hunting ground, him putting heads through walls, blackening my brother's eyes, choking me, swinging his belt, his shoe, his fist, whiskey spittle splashing into my big sister's watery eyes, her shitting her pants and the whole house buckling under the weight of him, was it that endless night, him screaming so help me god, I'll kill youz sons-of-bitches, was that the night I lost my land-legs, became a flopping fish and my sister became a scuttling, wingless bird, my brother mute as the startled-eyed dead bat we'd found belly up in the gutter, was it that night, the night that he screamed that someone, he didn't know who had left a smudge of dried oatmeal in a bowl, left it in the kitchen sink without washing it, without putting it away properly and he'd find out who dunnit if it was the last god-damned thing he did on god's good earth, he'd find out, he'd break us, worthless bitches, no good tramps, goddamn hoodlums, all of us, even the baby in his little crib, split lip, sore ass, diaper dangling around his chubby ankles and him wailing, the broken window glass sparkling like fallen stars and even Mary, Mother of God, and the Infant of Prague, toppled from the dresser, they were wide-eyed and watching him plow his way through to the morning, teaching us not to mock him, not to waste his hard-earned money, goddamn it, hadn't he'd had enough of us worthless piece of shits, didn't we ever learn, oh boy, you bet, he'd find out who dunnit; he'd find the rat, the dirty conniving, little thief who'd left an oatmeal smudge in a bowl in the kitchen sink after he'd told us once, no, he'd told us a thousand times that he wanted things put away properly, but oh no, bastards like us don't ever learn, so he'd have to teach us good-for-nothing shits if it took all night, this night, or any night or was it the night when the whole house buckled under the weight of summer's end that I lost myself, became a ghost?

Mary K O'Melveny
Empathy

As I lie in my hospital bed,
the indignities are unending.
Every body part lies open, flayed,
Yet I have become *third person.*
I am my *Chart,* my *PT Schedule.*
I am my *Bloodwork,* my *Vital Signs,*
my *X-ray Orders,* my *Sutures* and *Stitches.*
My room fills with strangers in green
and blue scrubs, eyes averted
as if my bed were unoccupied,
as if personal words might ignite
like firecrackers, each one lighting
up the next until flames fill the halls.
If only I could shout out my name
as firefighters try to save the building.

Still, hope curls up gently
next to me as I search
for fleeting moments where
we are not just a series
of pale bodies lined up
for tests and meds and meal trays,
metal tubes dangling
like unruly kudzu.
Where we might instead,
all together,
enjoy the sound
of a moaning trumpet
while we sit at a café table,
ice slowly melting
into our glasses of whiskey.

Tana Miller

A Poet Trapped in an Ant Colony

in the beginning   startled   thousands struggled to move her out
strong as they were   persistent   hard-working
they could not budge her heavy head   her size ten feet
amazed by her flesh   her hairy places   the pink of her tongue
they got down to basics   determined she was wingless   female
welcomed her in a limited way   politely
urged her to choose a suitable occupation for her stay
tend the eggs
feed the larvae
repair the nest
forage for food
pamper the queen
hurry hurry

but she refused to choose
I have thinking to do she stated
rhymes and lines to manage
I'm a POET for god's sake

the males didn't care what the poet did or didn't do
as they performed the one task males like best
in a never-ending delirious love fest
a cycle of create-new-life-die-soon-after
such was their bent   they were more than content

the queen didn't care about anything at all
she was a ferocious egg-machine
burning/churning day and night
born and bred to roll out eggs by the trillions
nothing else in her heart   her head

›

the witchy wingless females were the sticklers
they wanted the nest well-run
they insisted on rules   they loved regulations
they wanted things to be fair
they countenanced no slackers
the work must be shared   the work must be shared
they droned endlessly in the poet's ears and nose and hair
after ten years or so she threw down her pen
okay she screamed   at the end of her rope
I'm ready to crack
where is the queen
I'll care for her brood
I'll bring them their food
I'll coddle and swaddle and nurse
and forsake all verse
I promise to do what I ought

she made her voice cheerful
managed a stiff smirk
claimed she was a natural   a nurturer at heart
declared herself at peace   resigned to her lot
but in truth   dear reader   in truth
of course   absolutely   she was not

Mary K O'Melveny
Spit and Soot

James Charles Castle was a self-taught artist who was born deaf and mute in 1899. His work –
drawings, assemblages and books – were created almost exclusively on salvaged papers, packaging
materials and used food containers. Mixing his saliva with soot from the woodstove, Castle
created ink which he then applied using sharpened sticks and other found objects. Castle's
subjects ranged from people to building interiors and exteriors to animals and landscapes.
Recently, a new trove of Castle's artworks was discovered hidden in stairwells and rafters of his
former Idaho home, now a museum. Castle's work has been exhibited around the world.

I.

Ashes have piled up in our fireplace,
spilled ever so gently onto the hearth
as winter gasps and grapples with its end.

It does not occur to most that such grit
could represent more than memory's leavings
as fiery days cool down, that it could be

new language, tools of genius seeking
reincarnation as landscape, architectural grid,
word collage, humble portraiture.

II.

A simple farmhouse etched with broken
sticks of wood on cardboard box top.
The artist has spit into soot he has scraped

from a wood stove to make his ink.
He has scoured trash and ash heaps for bramble
scraps, seed pods, pen nibs, unclaimed mail.

With these tools and talismans, dirt and debris
devolve to diorama, mud to mural. His palette
is as wide and deep as earth's detritus.

III.

A graph of numbers and symbols
rich in secret meanings, a worn coat
with buttoned rows and hints of pockets.

Closets filled with boxes, shoes and windowed
corners, a sedan awaiting its driver, fences,
fields, tree lines crossed by wires and shadows.

Unable to speak or sign for his audience,
the artist holds their gaze with a touch of yellow
or red, a dangled wire or twisted string.

V.

On this frontier Idaho farm, words lost relevance.
The artifice of dialogue was easily dismissed
in favor of solid things a calloused hand could hold.

Each day, James gathered and gripped, ripped
and stripped, assembled and adorned, folded
and fondled his found objects. Saliva on slag.

As his stories emerged on odds and ends,
one imagines his family waiting in awe
as each new tale emerged from trash heaps.

VI.

Or perhaps they paid James no mind at all
as they observed him from afar, gathering
up his daily alphabet, their faces carved into

ironic smiles as he tended his flock of dispatches,
built his fences and outcrops, hiding some away
in dusty corners and shadowed stairwells.

Surely they would not have understood
that a trove of fireplace cinders could become
a Sistine Chapel.

Eileen Howard
Conversation

Conversation.
An apt word.
An adept at words
maybe misses....
Conversation.
       Communion
       Co-respondent
       Response
Dual bodies
in conversation...
Communion...
Collusion.
       Dual bodies
       responding,
       reading each other's
       fine lines....
       fat lines.
Lianas...
A bower of love.
       Fine lines
       Fat lines
       Frail lines
       Limned lines.
Limbs intertwined.
in conversation.

       Dialogue.
       An apt word.
       An adept at
       words,

maybe misses....
Conversation.

       Dialogue.....
       A dialing
       word
       for
       dual-dreams
       indemnity....
Joined in..
Engaged in...
Conversation.

Mary K O'Melveny

A Boy on a Bus

Looking up from folded up newspapers
and luminous cell phone screens,
passengers startle as whispers
are replaced by anguished keens,

a clamor jarring as blackboard chalk scrapers,
pitched just below jagged screams
of storm-ravaging winds. Day trippers
all, we are used to anything that seems

outlandish or hard -- mischief, capers
or tear-stained faces. We have seen
almost everything on this bus – slippers
and bathrobes; long legs that careen

like herons on stilettos; perfumed vapors
spilling over those who can't intervene;
pants hung so low they would embarrass drapers;
plastic wrapped patrons who definitely mean

to stay dry in rainstorms (practitioners
of hope's artistry who hold in esteem
memories of sunnier days); petitioners
with buttons, posters and flags carried between

limbs and on laps; harangues from earnest objectors;
babes in strollers and backpacks who seem
quite dismayed as extra baggage, their protectors'
faces impassive at the noisiness of our moving scene.

Still, sometimes complacency flickers
like summer fireflies, even when we mean
to keep our heads down, eyes blinkered.
These loud wails resonate like cut glass, their sheen

too luminous to ignore. Anxieties triggered,
we see the boy now. He is barely a teen.
Up, down, sideways, his head shakes with vigor.
Whisker fuzz on his chin belies his mien –

an infant lost in anguish. Only his mother
knows how to calm him, holding on so his lean
will not push him forward, pulling him to her
as his fetal position folds and unfolds. His citrine

eyes are hooded with fear. This ballet has feathered
her young face with delicate wrinkles. Between
each movement, his laments are as untethered
as a dissonant requiem. We imagine the mother's scene –

each day, her unsteady composer delivers
more notes. If the arc of her life was more routine,
she might adorn sheet music with these quivers
of sound, arrange them so they would be serene,

filled with joyousness. When they are discovered
in a velvet box in her closet – as she knows her son means
them to be heard some day – they will be calm as vespers,
filled with a sweetness that could not be foreseen.

Jan Zlotnik Schmidt

Vermeer's Lady Writing

She stares straight into our world
Her gaze penetrating centuries
A woman writing and waiting
Stories poised to be told
On her lips, by her hand
Fingers arched
She scorns the world's gaze
She is not a scribbling woman

Another girl in another time
Signs her name over and over
In aquamarine ink that bleeds
And smudges on white lined pages
She writes her name again and again
In cursive Jan Toby Zlotnik Jan Toby Zlotnik
Loops on the y on the z.....her own flourish

The name precedes her thoughts
The words and worlds she imagines
At night in a blue and white room
A stream of a street light filtering through blinds
She writes in invisible ink
All the stories she won't tell anyone
All the words she swallows
All the screeches in her head

She imagines her thoughts
Like starlings crashing against glass
Against window panes in a storm

Sometimes she draws swans' arched necks
Curved beaks black eyes
Swans drifting across an undammed stream
In the quiet she draws into herself

The woman in ermine and a lemon gold frock
Gazes at her across the centuries
The crowds in the museum disappear
The woman's words not yet formed
The gesture half finished

The woman and the girl reach across time
In the stillness of their longing.

RESISTANCE

Tana Miller

Speckled Egg

Leda had it all
a king for a father
a handsome warrior-husband
leisure to flaunt   her body
its moist places dawn rosy
lips breasts toes   juicy as berries
nipples spangled by afternoon sun

randy old Zeus   peered down from Olympus
a royal Peeping Tom   panting   sweating
disguised himself as a pure white cob
when he made his move
his fallen-angel wings filled the sky
beat against the summer heat
his hoarse whistles gave Leda scant warning
he landed on her   engulfed her
feathers filled her open-mouth-scream   her nose   eyes
his beak pried her legs apart
his long neck entered her
his wild grunts startled the world

I hold Zeus accountable for that afternoon
royalty's privilege provides no excuse
for intrusion   for violation
nor does a woman's beauty
no matter the ancients' self-serving assumptions

when Leda felt the swan's breast go limp
she turned her face and gasped for air
blood-drum beating in her ears
fingers curled into fists
after the great bird   depleted   departed
without a backward glance   her breath slowed
her body slackened
she placed her hands on her belly-swell
felt yeast bubbles rise within her dishonored womb
her yolk   surrounded by swan-egg-shell   pebble-small
that terrible day   but soon to sprout
half-mortal   half-divine   twins within one speckled egg
who would   in time   rock the world off its ancient axis

Jan Zlotnik Schmidt

A Gathering of Sybils: A Retelling

Once women gathered at the edge of
the sèa. They had albino skin, pink eyes,
scrawny limbs. They had lived hunched
in darkness in dark caves for many
centuries, eons too many to be named.
Examining their shadows on the wall.

And in air, tinged with salt and sea
spume, they tried to open their mouths
to speak, but only caws and squawks and
guttural sounds were heard. Yet this was
a beginning.

When they heard these sounds, they
looked at each other in fear. Closed their
eyes. Imagined words that couldn't be
heard. Only sensed in the silence.

They criss-crossed their arms against
their breasts, cursed their very being.
They knew Niobe's tears. Heard her
murmurs in the rock. They listened
for Philomena's cries. Whispers lodged
in their throats like seeds or splinters
of bone. Ready to be released. Words
stretching across a fog of white water.

Kit Goldpaugh

January 21, 2017:
A Poem in Two Voices

those who can march, do.

    cast on sixty pink stitches

nobody asked are you going

    knit three, purl two, knit two

we asked where, what time

    at the end of the row, purl three

by car, by bus, by train we come

    repeat the pattern of row one, starting with purl

gather in streets, parks, on bridges.

    repeat the pattern for four inches

we link arms, raise fists, and walk

    knit a row

mothers

    purl a row

daughters

    repeat for eight inches

granddaughters

    repeat pattern from first four inches

sisters

    cast off

in our pink pussy caps

    fold the knitting inside out
    stitch the sides together
    poke out the ears

march

Mary K O'Melveny

Portrait of a Gazan Stargazer

I am the proud son of a beggar.
I have never seen our ancestral
lands. I can reload my slingshot
with stones faster than olives drop
from the trees of my grandfather.
I have a scarf to cover up my
face when my eyes begin to sting
from tear gas or when burning
tire smoke catches in my throat.
I wrestle each day with barbed wire
as if it were a sordid thought
that could be swept from my mind's eye.
I have no job other than to
demand an end to the Nakba –
our forcible exile to lands
of no return. I have little
use for prayer and cannot bear
the cost of love. Our kitchen floor
is made of sand. I can build a fire
to cook eggplants and tomatoes.
I used to raise birds on our roof –
chickens and pigeons – but my winged
companions were soon felled by bombs.
To replace them, I learned to make
kites from plastic bags and paper
strips that can sail across fences
and berms to carry our messages.
I like to sleep in the desert
where star patterns suggest an open world.
I try to imagine how I would
traverse its pathways, my arms wide,
my voice filled with songs of longing.

An April 30, 2018 story by New York Times reporters, Iyad Abuheweila and David M. Halbfinger,
recount an interview with 22 year-old Gaza City resident Saber al-Gerim whose days are spent
lobbing rocks at Israeli soldiers over the prison-like border fence.

It doesn't matter if they shoot me or not, Mr. al-Gerim said. *Death or life — it's the same thing.*

Kappa Waugh

Death's Door

Death's door surprised me
peeling blue paint,
crappy wreath
of plastic daisies, plus the
door was clearly hollow core.
The Grim Reaper needs
to watch more HGTV,
I thought. Get an upgrade.
Make it pop in matte black
with brushed nickel fixtures.
No doorbell in sight,
not even a knocker.
The welcome mat
uninviting, outdated.

So I walked away.

Mary K O'Melveny

Six minutes, 20 Seconds

Emma stands
resolute
calm before millions
crowds begin
to shift
uneasily
uncertainly
to look around
to feel how long it is
to wonder
as moments slip by
like lives lost
lives altered
by pain
by fury
by disbelief
by finality
just how it would feel
lying under a desk
stuffed in a closet
covered in classmates' blood
surrounded by downed friends, teachers
how it would be
to hear jagged sounds
burst from all directions
to have no exit
to see no future
to lose all faith

Emma does not move
she is still counting
each second
is a lifetime lost
she knows how
it will end
she knows
what we need to do
she shows us our power
to take action
even when time
is short
even when time
is stalled, stilled
Emma knows
time's truths
she will make us see
tears
terror
travesty
with each
tick tick tick
she will make us hear
an AK 15
again and again
for six minutes, 20 seconds

*On March 24, 2018, Emma Gonzalez, a survivor
of the Parkland, Florida school massacre, held
crowds spellbound for six minutes, 20 seconds
of silence – the time it took the shooter to kill
17 students and wound 15 others.*

Kappa Waugh

Man's Best Friend

There is a Dutch word, "doordringend," which means through-piercing. That was the sound of the dog barking on a July afternoon when I was twelve. The windows were open because it was hot, and we had no air conditioning. My mother, who told us frequently that she was a great poet, was trying to write in her bedroom, which looked onto the backyard. From the far end of the yard, but out of sight, came the dog's persistent bark. It had reached that hysterical high pitch, only matched by a baby's cry, that makes the hearer think, "Surely they will wear themselves out soon, and we will get some peace." Meanwhile, the dog, or baby, is feeling, "I will go on making this hopeless, unhappy cry for all eternity. Misery at top pitch is all I can utter."

First it is important to know that my mother hated dogs. A few individual animals she met were not totally despised, but in general, her dog descriptors were "loathsome," "vile," "craven." Three years earlier, as she drove through Little Rock, Arkansas, we children were sure she had hit a dog in the road. Not only did she refuse to turn back and check, but claimed there was no dog, and if there was, it shouldn't have been loose, and so deserved any glancing blow it might have received. In later years, when we accused her of killing a dog in Little Rock, she would roll her eyes and say, "Oh, you children always exaggerate so."

Another time my mother and I went to a folk festival in England. We sat in a tent, in the front row and were enjoying the first of the storytellers when a dog strolled up and settled itself near my mother's feet. "Go away!" she hissed at it, but instead it raised its hind leg and started that doggy personal grooming. The sound effects were incredible. "TOK, TOK, TOK," slurped his tongue against his privates. My mother pushed at him with her foot, trying to roll him over and send him on his way. He only looked at her reproachfully, and went back to his toilette. The storyteller was distracted by this competition. His eyes slewed toward her and away again. By now, my mother was kicking the dog vigorously with her foot while watching the speaker with a courteous, interested look. Her disconnect was total. The storyteller dropped the thread of his narrative, slowed, started up again like an old windup phonograph. The more his eyes were drawn to the combatants, the more ragged his tale became, until finally he stopped dead. At that point, my mother struck out so vigorously at the dog, she unbalanced and fell off her chair, sprawling next to her nemesis as if they were littermates. The dog, which had borne her attentions quite patiently, clearly found this development distressing, for he started to bark great hoarse barks.

Well, I have leapt way ahead of that July day I started on, but you now have a clearer sense of my mother's relationship to dogs.

So the barking was disturbing my mother's writing time, and, somewhat like Henry II speaking of Thomas Becket, she cried out, "Who will rid me of this nightmare hound? I'll give them ten bucks." I went out to the end of the yard, looked through the fence and greenery between our yard and the dog's. I could see that he was tied up and had wound himself so thoroughly around the tree that he couldn't reach shade or his water. I didn't free him immediately, but went back to the house and called up the stairs to my mother, "Where do we keep the ax?" I was feeling that it would be too simple to merely free the dog; my mother deserved more for her money. "In the garage," she answered. "Why?" "Don't ask," was my reply.

Next I walked around the block to the neighbor's property, and made my way to their backyard. Speaking kindly to the dog, I unwound him, though leaving him tied up. He drank, lay down in the shade, and gave a great sigh. The silence was bliss.

At home again, I went to collect my fee. "What did you do?" asked my mother, who had finally made a connection between the dog's silence and my ax question. "You don't want to know. Never ask me again," I answered sternly. Every few years after that she looked at me a bit nervously and asked, "Did you really kill that dog?" For her seventy-fifth birthday present, I told her the true story.

Mary K O'Melveny

Kindness

Some of us are trying to be *kind*.
Even in smallest ways. Even as the known
world self-destructs around us, shards of
optimism falling from the sky before we even
have a chance to look up to see what has
shifted us off our comfortable axis.

I've got a chipmunk problem in my yard.
The tiny furred creatures have popped up
everywhere, sending showers of dirt
into the air like it was Yellowstone.
I cannot kill them even though I want to.
They will not leave even though I have raged

at them, insulted them and their ancestors.
My neighbor brings a *Havahart* trap
so I can remove them kindly. He baits it with
peanut butter. Soon the trap has a frightened
occupant. I cannot bear to look out for fear
of crying. The prisoner is soon relocated.

The trap is replaced. A new chipmunk takes
the bait. He too is repatriated to a new territory.
Capture and repeat. The metal trap looms larger
each day as an unending array of innocents are
tempted by creamy nut paste. Soon enough,
I begin to worry about babes left behind in tunnels,

about mothers and fathers grieving for lost children.
One day a chipmunk plants itself on my deck
and looks in through the window. My *kind* self
huddles behind the blind. I will not make eye contact.
This is the *humane* way, I say to myself, even as I begin
to imagine each trapped rodent wearing an orange

jumpsuit as interrogators gather nearby with pen
and paper waiting for the inevitable confessions.
One night, the trap is sprung, its detainee freed from
house arrest. I am thrilled. Then I learn that a bear
has likely done it. Probably thanked me for the easy meal.
Now I am lost in my worst fears. There is no *kindness* in my yard.

How could I have thought otherwise? This is how
it always begins. Good intentions vanishing
like some dying star, rationalizations
reverberating across celestial centuries.
Turns out it is our unwavering belief
in our self-righteousness that is the trap.

Colleen Geraghty
Showcase of Sacrifice

I've given blood a couple of times but never donated a kidney,
never given a piece of my liver, never served water to the thirsty
from the jawbone of an ass.
But, you call on Sunday from the borderland
between pop-psychology and neuroscience, rhapsodize
about my pathological altruism, my over-giving,
co-dependent, people-pleasing, low-self-esteem,
breeding prodigalism.

You diagnose me with Mother Teresa Syndrome,
declare my giving 'until it hurts,' a sign of mental derangement.
My reckless generosity, like a bot fly,
has wormed into your craw, festered
like a relentless addiction to indignation, and on a Sunday,
sweet with milky twilight, you drown me
and my giving
in a sea of obstinate dogmatism.

Thrown overboard in the maelstrom of your projections,
I am reduced to pathology,
diagnosed a spectral empath,
a reckless giver
who hides her own needs,
denies them,
pretends they do not exist.

If I'd gotten my day in your court,
I'd have shown you that I am no showcase of self-sacrifice.
I do not use giving as compensation
for what I've never gotten.
I'm no fierce angel shouldering the dead,
no bountiful mother letting prisoners
suckle milk from my tits.

If you could have seen me through the film of your own story,
you might have discovered that I am nothing
Caravaggio would have immortalized.

I am an ordinary woman
who once walked the procession of the living dead, a mere mortal
who now finds grace in thigh-deep snow, inside the big house
across the driveway, where a dying old woman, with goosebumps
shivering down her legs, calls for me, shouting, "Come, please!
My feet are swollen. I can't get my pants up."

Landlocked in an unexpected March blizzard,
I put the old woman's needs first,
pummeled through heavy snow for her.
If you'd taken a breath,
shut your mouth for five minutes,
I could have shared the pleasure
I'd taken from holding her feet,
her toes purple as magnolia flowers,
blossoming in my winter hands,
the skin on her blue-veined legs
thin as rice paper.

No, I didn't have the balance sheet for the debt
you'd said I was owed in return for what I'd given.
What I got
from the hive of her old lips
was richer than honey –
stories brighter than sunlight
on the stormiest of days.
I got one last chance to serve her
hot soup made from a chicken
my daughter had slaughtered
with her own, strong, young hands.

RESILIENCE

Colleen Geraghty
The Beer House

There are some people born to booze it up, oozing booze, breathing the boozy all over you no matter what time of day or night.

We knew how to *tie-one-on*. For Christ's sake, even the babies knew how to *tie-one-on* especially during those times when he was popping-in to Murphy's Pub or Finnegan's Dance Hall or Fogarty's Tap Room or that beer joint off the highway where those fat-assed German ladies served up bratwurst and sauerkraut and beer. He'd pull over, stopping-by and popping-in to this place or that place, or the other place. He'd holler for us to shut the hell up, roll down the windows half an inch, grind his smoking butt under the heel of his boot and yell, "Lock the damn doors, and don't talk to nobody, you hear. I'll kill you sons-of-bitches if you start any shit."

Sometimes he'd slap my brother silly all over his skinny damn arms and scream, "That's a taste of what's coming for you if you start any of your crap." My sister would turn to milk, all white like magnesia. She always blanched on a night of popping-in. Took her awhile to warm up to the fun. Her in the back seat praying that she'd put a damn diaper and a couple of teething biscuits into a bag cause one of them babies was sure to shit themselves, squawk it up good. He'd welt my sister's no-good ass when she forgot what was good for her. Popping-in, stopping-by, and tying one-on was

a concentrating kind of a thing and he didn't want to be bothered with kid crap or baby crap or any kind of crap when he was in his swinging-by kinda mood.

Some nights we'd clear forget about him, forget about the boozy, the popping-in, stopping-by, beer joint of it all, and we'd really tie-one-on, raise a whole lot of fun out there in the car, playing taxi. Hopping back and forth over the seat. My brother hollering, "Lady, Lady, where you going?" My sister hollering back, "Macy's" or "Gimbels." Sometimes, she'd act the snooty lady and shout, "John Wanamaker's." My brother, with a butt in his mouth, would call back, "Ok ladies, your pleasure." He always took to being the cabby, shoving an old ashtray butt into his mouth and flicking his ash like he was born to it. We were the ladies, usually rich Main Line bitches with fancy shoes and manners galore. My little sisters were the maids, some poor service girls we dragged around with us to carry our packages. God knows, when you're rich, you can barely wipe your own ass, let alone carry expensive shit around by yourself.

One time we were robbers in a getaway car but that didn't last long. Halfway through the shoot up my brother started belly-aching and hollering, "You stupid bitches, getaway cars don't got no babies in them." And my sister, who had enough of him always being in the front seat, hollered, "Shut up, you ain't the boss of us." Diving for her like a crow dives for a dead cat, my brother gotta hold of her hair, came up with a fist full of clumps. "Shut up, you no-good-bitch, before I kill you."

My little sister started bawling which set the babies off and pretty soon it seemed we were all cold. Freezing half to death with the night air seeping under the window crack, the car lights whizzing by us in the dark. All of us staring into the German House of Beer, wondering just how long this popping-in, stopping-by, tying-one on with his friends was gonna take. Taxi was fun and gangster woulda been too if my brother hadn't reminded us what a mess a baby can be. After all, who can have a proper shoot up with a diaper full of shit?

One time we made it all the way to France out there, right in front of the Beer House. We were playing Charles Lindbergh. You know, the one where he shoved his whole family into his special airplane and flew them all the way across the Atlantic just so he could bury a couple of his kids in some French meadow. Everybody knew he was sick and tired of feeding them brats, always being broke. My brother was Mr. Lindbergh, holding my Buster Brown to my big sister's head like it was his tough gun, whispering like a frog. "Gimme them babies, Martha, we're going to France." Martha put up such a fuss he had to clunk her. Tied her hands behind her back with my shoe laces. "Shut your hole woman, quit your squawking, we got enough damn kids already." And Martha cried and prayed to every French saint she knew until Charles had enough of her belly-aching and he was forced to gag her, just to shut her trap.

That night we flew clear to France. All the way across the Atlantic. Mr. Lindbergh flying us right up and over that ocean. All the kids and Martha bound and gagged. Mr. Lindbergh singing songs of praise for European meadows and how much we'd love them. Not one baby ever suspecting what was coming for them. Only Martha getting that he was fed up as fed up can be -- not enough to go around. That night flew by fast. France waiting on us. Charles acting the tough-guy. Martha struggling to free herself. Flying over that ocean, we didn't hardly notice the dark. Forgot all about the House of Beer. Didn't feel the damp or the cold night kicking our asses around the car. Too busy tying-one-on. We fell asleep in the fun of that plane, forgetting everything in the world except flying.

We didn't hardly notice when he came stumbling out of his German House of Beer, opening the car door, belching-it-up-good. Beer and bratwurst, pretzels and whatever else slopping out, splashing down the side of my brother's sleepy arm, splattered into my sister's hair. All of us waking up cold. My sister crying, wiping his chewed-up slop outa her eyes, off her shirt, her hair stinking now, swinging wet down the back of her Sunday dress. Him oozing booze and too far gone to notice that Mr. Lindbergh had flown us all the way to France. Him too tied-up with his good time splattering to notice that he'd up-chucked all over the most famous flying gangster of all time. Charles Lindbergh flying us all the way to France. It was a damn gooey mess to untangle them stinky laces from around my sister's sleepy splattered wrists. We used a wet diaper to wipe her off and my brother whispered, "Quit your whining, there ain't no shit in this one."

Leave it to Himself to wreck a plane ride, belching and slobbering his popping-in, stopping-by, tying-one-on, German good time all over us. Bratwurst and beer, sauerkraut and pretzel mustard, him slobbering that whole mess all down the side of the car, stinking right into our sleepy French eyes. My sister's hair plastered and sticky, dripping every German belly-aching thing all over her skin like she hadn't had enough already just being married to Charles Lindbergh.

Even if he did bury us under a mountain of German slop, the good part of all his popping-in was that we got to fly clear to France and back again. After all the flying and the slobbering stench, we got to see the sun come up over Philly. The whole place quiet and steamy - watery veils of light falling all over the city. Getting home in time for cereal. Popping-in wasn't half bad if you could forget about the slobbering. If you could forget about the cold.

Jan Zlotnik Schmidt

Punta Mujeres: A Land of Grief

This is a land scorched
by fire, pumice, and flame,
charred lava rocks that lead down to the sea

This is a land where old women
shuffle slowly and look directly
into cloudless skies

And they beckon to us
point to small green and purple figs
offerings wrinkled as they are

This is the land of old women
who mince their steps
mouth words through the gaps in their teeth

Their words betray no doubt
No shame in aging
or keening

They birth ten or twelve
Gather them in the folds of their dresses
 like lost letters

They know the power of tides
the tormentas, the calima
The power to destroy

And they walk in
their own shadows
forsaken angels.

Kit Goldpaugh

Wallpapering with Mom

The house that I grew up in is the same house that my mother grew up in. She moved in when she was three and stayed for the next seventy years. Then she died. In the meantime, she taught herself, among other things, to wallpaper.

When we were growing up, the house was settling. That meant that there was a hill in the dining room floor, cracks in the walls, and when my mother took up wallpapering during her Early American period, the Revolutionary War soldiers in the living room were sliced to full decapitation where the ceiling met the wall. That was only if the paper was hanging straight. When the soldiers stood erect and kept their heads, the entire room slanted just enough to make a guest uneasy.

Ethel Murphy from work told my mother that wallpaper would cover all those old cracks and water stains so Mom decided to wallpaper the house, one room at a time, beginning with the worst room, mine. First though, she read the DIY book that Mrs. Murphy brought to work for her. She laid the book open on the kitchen table, lit a Camel unfiltered and taught herself to wallpaper. My sister Shelley and I joined her at the table. That night, we learned about plumb bobs and plumb lines. We learned about pattern matches and pattern drops. We learned that vinyl paper is easier to apply because it doesn't tear as easily as wallpaper. Pre-pasted paper is even

easier and less messy than that. Some information was from the book, and some was from Mrs. Murphy who called at 7:30 for a Q & A. Shelley and I helped to calculate the area of the room, and the number of rolls of paper we would need, allowing for a generous pattern drop. We would need ten double rolls or twenty single. Mom hoped that they would find enough matching rolls to paper my room. She and Mrs. Murphy were going to The Fishkill Wallpaper Outlet.

On Saturday afternoon, my mother came home with several rolls of vinyl, pre-pasted wallpaper and Mrs. Murphy's wallpapering tools. At the outlet, she and Mrs. Murphy had gone to, they only carried discontinued patterns or slightly defective paper or both. The paper that they chose for my room fell into both categories, making it deeply discounted. It was a pink floral design my mother said, dropping the first box of not pink, but a decidedly salmon colored pattern on a white background. There were nine rolls of pre-pasted vinyl paper. A couple of the rolls were slightly lighter or darker than the others, thus that deep discount. That night, Mom sized the walls. Sunday was wallpaper day.

Since the pattern was an overall design, my mother reasoned, matching patterns would not be an issue at all as there was nothing to match. She measured and precut four pieces of paper. She soaked the first rolled piece in a long plastic trough on the bed to loosen the paste. The book had said to hang the first piece overlapping a corner by an inch. That proved too difficult so my mother pasted the first piece right at the edge, not around the corner. It took most of the day to cover the first two walls which had no windows or doors. When she reached the corner, she cut the paper to the end of the wall. The next wall was a new start. She cut and patched around the windows. Once she had to discard most of a roll because a yard of the flowers had bled. Another roll had bleached spots. If a defect was not obvious, the paper stayed. Sometimes, Mom would cut out the ruined paper and patch together another section of wall. But still, with only one-half wall to go, she ran out of wallpaper.

"I have an idea," she said, crushing her cigarette in a tuna can. "We'll put up an accent wall."

The next Saturday, Mom went alone to Pittsburgh Paints and headed for the discount bins of paper in the back. She wasn't going to drive all the way to Fishkill just for a couple of rolls of paper, she said. She came home with three rolls of paper for her accent wall. Apparently, she had relied on her memory for color and design when she chose a paper to complement the original "pink." It was striped pink leaning more toward lavender than peach, not even close to salmon. Nevertheless, up it went with the same disregard for matching as the rest of the room. Some stripes were wider than

others, some slanted. We looked around the finished room. The effect was slightly jarring.

"I think that piece is upside down," I said.

My mother lit a cigarette. "Nobody will notice."

"OK," I said. It was understood that nobody would notice the bubbles and sharply cut corners or the ragged tops of each piece, either. Mom must have noticed my disappointment. She offered, "We could cut the striped paper lengthwise and make a border."

Room by room, mom met her goal. She loved the wallpaper outlet. Eagles and little flags and guns covered the walls of the house, all right side up. She never did quite master the art of matching patterns exactly so there were sometimes soldiers with dislocated shoulders and little gaps in their guns. Her last project was a plaid dining room, now a den, still on a hill. Plaid.

What Mrs. Murphy neglected to tell my mother was that what goes up must come down and that removing wallpaper, while less precise a task, is a more difficult one than putting it up. The wallpaper on O'Reilly St. stayed up for the next family to enjoy many years later.

Forty years later, when my son prepared to paint my room, he faced a wall of gardenias, an accent, reminiscent of the old castle.

"Can we paint over the paper?"

"I don't think so."

"Have you ever used a steamer?"

"Yeah, but maybe we can avoid it. This looks like it should come down pretty easily."

"When Buddy and I removed paper last summer, we used vinegar and water."

"OK. Let's try that."

Standing on a step-stool, Matt said, "I'll go high, you go low."

We scored and sprayed vinegar and water as well as the brand name remover all over the gardenias. It made no difference. The gardenias clung to the wall. As each pin prick soaked in the liquid, the wall looked like a BBC map of a malaria outbreak. Spray, wait, scrape. Repeat. The first day, we played show tunes, nice lively stuff to keep us moving. I sang. I defied gravity. I fought the French Revolution and won and lost in love over and over. The second day, we switched to hip-hop and rap, Matt's choice.

"I wish you had a different bucket list," said Matt. "Why can't you just want to go Kenya or the Galapagos or something?"

"It's because I'm not delicate," I lamented. "If I were delicate, I wouldn't be expected to scrape wallpaper or hike for miles or raise a pit-bull. I could act like the senior citizen that I am and tend a few geraniums and rock on the porch with a chihuahua."

"No, Ma. You aren't delicate. Sorry.

Tough. Ropey. That's you."

I sigh. Spray, wait, scrape.

The third day, I woke before light. I didn't even change my clothes but went right to work in my pajamas. I sprayed a section of the wall in the vinegar mix and crawled downstairs to flip the switch on the coffee. By the time the coffee was ready, so was the wall. High on caffeine and determination, I scraped and scraped, sometimes too vigorously, sending little pieces of sheetrock flying.

No more Gilbert and Sullivan, no Wu Tang; today was a day for a dirge. I sang lyrics of America's song "A Horse With No Name." I sang along,

When the song reached the ninth day where he let the horse run free, I let this horse run free, too. It happened when Matt arrived at 8:00 a.m. "Stop," he said, "I don't want to have to sheetrock."

An Amazon box sat smiling on the porch two days later. In it were four double rolls of textured wallpaper, designed like a tin ceiling of six-inch squares. "This stuff will cover bullet holes and fist punches, and it's meant to be painted," said Matt.

Matt worked nothing like my mother. Instead of a blue chalk plumb line, Matt used a laser, a bright red line that left no blue fingerprints all over the wall and woodwork like a crime scene the way Mom's did. Only after carefully matching patterns did he lay each strip of paper over a piece of plywood on sawhorses and opened the paste. Mom had just worked right off the bed, made or unmade. Matt brushed the paste evenly, not lifting the brush far from the paper. When Mom "slapped on" the paste, little lumps flew everywhere and stuck on walls, the bedsheets, the floor and the wallpaper. For weeks, I'd find little scraps of paper everywhere in my room. For years after each project, tiny scraps of paper remained glued to the floors and woodwork of every room.

Once he had hung the first piece, Matt said, "You can go." Oh, the tricks of the trade that his grandmother could have taught him.

Eileen Howard

Hiking Montana

Solomon's seal,
gay feather,
wild columbine,
combine in an
azure blue
startlingly clear
ambient
mountain moan.

Rips the river,
through gouged
rock... Rock
tumbled
errantly,
gigantically,
elementally
around...

Astounded
(astonished)
A few tenacious
pines
have flung
themselves
up out of
sheer rock.

Flaunting their
thick green needles,
they fling
their tops proudly
over barren terrain:
jumbled
dense-solid
rock.

Determined

adamant
they assert
their
presence.

Their roots
drill out sustenance
through
the stony heart
of the tumbled
mountain.

And the
columbine
flowers sweetly
in a rock
rook-nook,
Buddha-wise:
in a small
cavern
in
a whisper
of soil.

Tana Miller

Hemerocallis Fulva (Beauty for a Day)

I crawl on my belly from spot to spot
ferreting out ditch lily rhizomes
snout to the ground
a pig hunting truffles
find one   heartlessly hack
it to death   on to another
I have waged war for thirty years
against the slutty plant
intent on colonizing my garden
H. fulva is a vulgar girl
mother always warned me
against taking up with the likes of her
too sexy she'd say   and I promise you
her underwear's not clean
and all those children!
poor things aren't real lilies at all
pretenders she spits   purses her lips
and orange of all colors!
ever oppositional   I invite H. fulva into my yard anyway
I had nothing cheerful growing there
no money for the nursery
so one spring day I grabbed a spade
raided the roadsides
dug her up   brought her home
coddled her pale hairy roots
her lumpy nether parts
for a few years she simpered
and swayed   well-behaved
covered her swollen genitals
with modest sword-like leaves
in June she bloomed
bawdy and bold   blatantly orange   but
since each hussy blossom died in a day
my senses remained intact
a gift   I felt grateful
I didn't realize then: nothing is free
reader   that nasty girl spread and spread
overground   underground
H. fulva took over my yard

Eileen Howard
Yellowstone Hot Springs

Out of fissures
erupts or oozes
bubbling hot water
forged in earth's cauldron:
ebbs and flows,
roils and gurgles.

Gargantuan
gray mud balloons,
erupt in slow motion.
Dragon hot springs
fling transparent
teardrops in your face.

Strange life forms
emerge
luminescent
limpid. Impossible
wild colors
jostle and shout.

Old rust,
vivid cerise,
brilliant turquoise,
atomic tangerine
emerge in patterns
of streamers and mats.

Some sulfurous, some
not. Some fermenting,
some not. Formed by bacteria,
arcane and mysterious.
Aligned and
reflecting prisms of light.

A black bird, unfazed,
braves the heat
to feed on what:
A strange life form:
an exotic thermophile
that thrives in a
mud furnace?

Kappa Waugh
Holy Martyrs

On the day the game "Holy Martyrs" was born, Sister Mercita had told the second grade about the Blessed Perpetua, who was slain by wild beasts. "They rent her from limb to limb, children. Her lifeblood made the earth all around turn crimson, but she never wavered in her faith. Saint Perpetua continued to pray with her last breath. Pray for that kind of fortitude, girls and boys."

Mary Beth asked Sister Mercita what kinds of beasts they were. Sister Mercita thought lions and tigers. Ann Comely said, "What about catamounts and panthers?" Yes, Sister felt certain that catamounts and panthers were among the animals that had savaged the Blessed Perpetua. Caswell was straining in his seat, waving his hand. When Sister called on him, he stood and asked, "Did the beasts bite Blessed Perpetua's head off?"

"Yes, Caswell. Eventually."

"Well, S-Sister," Caswell was almost stuttering with excitement. "C-c-could her head keep praying when it was bitten off?"

Marguerite and Bennett burst out in nervous laughter; Marguerite continued laughing and gasping till it turned to hiccups, and she had to be excused to the drinking fountain. Carter raised his hand, and, when Sister Mercita called on him, wanted to know if wolves were included.

Sister Mercita's eyes narrowed, and she had the little roll of flesh above the bridge of her nose that meant she was becoming fed up. "No more questions, children. It is not important whether there were elephants or guinea pigs present at the Blessed Perpetua's martyrdom!" The children darted looks at each other. Guinea pigs and elephants had never occurred to them. "What is important is that this blessed martyr met a terrible death with joy and reverence because she was sustained by God and His angels."

At recess Katharine suggested, "Let's play St. Perpetua." While a group of second graders gathered near the big rock on the playground, Katharine explained the rules. "We'll count off for who'll be It, that is Perpetua. The rest of us will bite them with our sharp teeth and rend them with our fierce claws _ not hard, of course."

"And the Saint has to keep praying the whole time, right?" added Billy.

"Yes, and you can only bite between the elbow and the wrist," improvised Katharine, who lived in dread of anyone's discovering that she was terribly ticklish. "Because then we can cover any marks with our sleeves."

"You said no hard bites or scratches. You promised!" squeaked Laura.

"Well, I know, but what if Hamlet sneezed accidentally when he was biting, and it made him bite down? It wouldn't be cheating, his breaking the rules, but it might happen." "Or you might trip, just at the second you went to claw her," suggested Loretta.

"Yes.""Or maybe," Hamlet looked pleased, "a bank robber could come by, shooting his gun, and get you startled." "Yes, yes, YES!" snapped Katharine, "Can't we just start playing now!"

So they counted off, "Eeny, meeny, miney, moe," and at "very last ONE," Katharine was it. "No fair," she whispered. "I thought of the game. It's my game! I shouldn't have to be It."

Hamlet looked at the others, then looked directly at Katharine, right into her eyes, saying "That's why you have to be the Blessed Martyr, Katharine. To show us the way. Besides, we'll never play with you again if you don't play fair. You started this."

Katharine looked at the dozen children watching her. With her back against the rock, she brushed her fingers back and forth against its roughness. Small grains of stone came loose. She looked down. One of her knee socks had collapsed in wrinkles. "Ok," she whispered, then loudly, "OK!" She began unbuttoning her cuffs and rolling up her sleeves. Her forearms looked so white to her; the hairs were standing up, even though it was a warm day.

"Hamlet took on the role of head pagan. "St. Perpetua, give up your God, stop telling us about Jesus and His Mother, and eat this baloney sandwich, even though it's Friday."

"Never!" yelled Katharine, rolling her eyes heavenward.

"Then we'll have to send in wild beasts to eat you alive. Right, fellow pagans?"

"Right!" the second graders shouted.

Katharine remained standing against the rock, her arms stuck straight out beside her, forearms bared. Hamlet formed the others into two rows behind a line he kicked in the dirt. "We'll take turns; first one beast will savage one side of Blessed Perpetua, then the next beast will take the other arm." He turned to Katharine, "You better start praying to that God of yours, Perpetua."

Which prayer should she say, Katharine wondered? Hail Mary was shorter, Our Father was longer. She wasn't sure she could remember all the Apostle's Creed or the Act of Contrition.

"OUR FATHER WHICH ART IN HEAVEN..." Laura came forward, growling softly, and scratched delicately at Katharine's arm. Then, looking at Katharine sideways through her fall of blond hair, she gave her the lightest of nips.

"HALLOWED BE THY NAME..." On her other side, Loretta made big clawing gestures, but barely touched her arm. Her roaring noises and the evil face she was making were scary. Loretta bared her teeth ferociously, and, as she plunged her face down, Katharine tensed, but never felt any teeth. Loretta was using her hair to hide the fact that she wasn't biting at all! "Oh, Loretta," silently vowed Katharine, "I'll always pick you first for kickball."

Becky Lou marched up next, hissing, as Katharine continued, "THY KINGDOM COME, THY WILL BE DONE..." Becky had sharp teeth, and she ate dirty food like dog biscuits and lard. Katharine hoped the bite wouldn't fester. Her father said human bites were the dirtiest. But Becky didn't bite down hard at all.

"ON EARTH AS IT IS IN HEAVEN..." Here comes Bennett Thorpe-the-Twerp," thought Katharine, "snorting and snuffling." Again, the bite was painless, but his scratching hurt for a second. "Still," thought Katharine, "this is easier than I thought. Ann Comely's next, and I'm almost halfway through."

"GIVE US THIS DAY OUR DAILY BREA..." Ann Comely snarled and struck at the air as she rocked from foot to foot directly in front of Katharine. "Give me your snack tomorrow, and I won't hurt you." Ann's voice was low. Katharine gave a tiny nod, and Ann made chewing noises while pretending to bite and worry Katharine's arm.

"AND FORGIVE US OUR TRESPASSES..." Carter Ward came prancing forward making a wolf howl. He grabbed Katharine's arm and twisted in opposite directions, giving her a painful Indian burn. As he brought his mouth to her skin, she was afraid; then her stomach flopped as she realized he was licking her arm instead of biting it. His tongue burned against her wrist. He put his face close to hers, winked, then uttered his wolf howl again. Katharine stared at Carter, her mouth agape. Was that dirty, or was it nice? She was suddenly afraid she needed to pee.

"Pray! Blessed Saint Perpetua," called Hamlet sternly, "Or you aren't a holy Christian martyr!"

"Pray!" echoed the others.

"AS WE FORGIVE THOSE ..." Katharine's concentration was wavering. What had Carter meant by that? Did he want to be mean or friends? Oh, good, Billy was next. He was her friend, her next-door-neighbor. "AS WE FORGIVE THOSE.." "Kir KirKir!" Billy was like a small, fierce bird, cawing and soaring his arms as he flew toward her. Katharine smiled at Billy as she finished the phrase, "WHO TRESPASS AGAINST US.." Billy brushed her arms with his fingertips, then bit her. Hard! Katharine flinched, astonished; her eyes began to water, and she cried out, "Billy!"

"I sneezed," claimed Billy, grinning at her over his shoulder as he ran back to Hamlet's side of the line. Katharine's arm showed an oval of toothmarks.

"I'll get him," Katharine vowed. "I'll tell my brother that Billy was the one who stole his penny collection. And spent it on sherbet at High's Ice Cream."

"AND LEAD US NOT INTO TEMPTATION..." MaryBeth danced forward. She looked like a fox with her red hair and bright green eyes. She yipped, barked, and scratched Katharine while giving her a short, sharp nip. "BUT DELIVER US FROM EVIL..." Caswell Harris was up next, and Katharine hated him totally. He told awful, sickening lies _ you hoped they were lies. He said he sucked his little sister's titty and milk had come out. He said he drank the blood when his father chopped the head off their Sunday chicken. He said daddies put their peepee in mommies and that made babies. Caswell walked up in total silence, put his two hands on the rock above her shoulders, and leaned in smirking toward her face. Caswell was so close Katharine could see a tiny line of white hairs in one eyebrow. Katharine pressed back into the rock and twisted her head to catch Hamlet's eye. Hamlet called out, "Just the arm, Caswell." Caswell smiled at Katharine and laid his cheek against her forearm. Taking a small pinch of skin between his eye teeth, he bore down, moving the teeth back and forth as he continued to watch her intently, smiling. She felt like throwing up! The pain was bad, but Caswell's smile was worse. She wouldn't cry! Her tears would please him too much. She gritted her teeth and turned her head to Hamlet again. "Hamlet! Caswell's cheating!

He's really hurting!" Her voice rose, quavering, and she kicked Caswell in the shin, just as he stopped biting her. He still smiled as he turned away to join the others.

"HAIL MARY, FULL OF GRACE! THE LORD IS WITH THEE..." Katharine's voice was shaky, and she didn't dare look at her arm where Caswell had bitten her. Marguerite Moon ran up, flailing and hooting, pretending to claw her.

"BLESSED ART THOU AMONG WOMEN..." Marguerite opened her mouth on Katharine's arm without closing her big, square teeth. Her parents and Katharine's were friends, and the two girls spent Wednesday afternoons together while their moms were den mothers for Cub Scouts.

"AND BLESSED IS THE FRUIT OF THY WOMB, JESUS..." Marguerite had underpants with the days of the week embroidered on them in cursive script, Katharine knew. Today she was probably wearing" Thursday." Thursday was lavender.

"HOLY MARY, MOTHER OF GOD..." Hamlet, chief pagan, the last of the wild beasts, threw himself into it, weaving before Katharine with growls and feints. He curled his fingers into claws and drew them firmly along the length of the arm Caswell had just bitten.

"PRAY FOR US SINNERS.." Why didn't it hurt, Katharine wondered? Was it a miracle? Did God take away the pain from His martyrs if they were faithful to the end? She glanced at Hamlet's hand. Of course! Hamlet bit his nails! There was only a thick bulb of flesh at the end of each finger.

"NOW AND AT THE HOUR OF OUR DEATH..." Hamlet's bite, when it came, was a firm pressing of his mouth against her arm.

Katharine looked over his back at the others. Loretta, Bennett, and Billy were still being savage animals, tossing their heads and striking at the air. The other children watched Hamlet and Katharine.

"AMEN! AMEN!" sang out Katharine, bursting away from Hamlet, the rock, from martyrdom, from her classmates. With a beatific smile, she raced for the school door, leaping and bounding, almost airborne in light.

Later in the afternoon, when Katharine remembered to look at her arm, she saw only two small dents, as if she had been bitten by a snake.

TRANSFORMATIO

Jan Zlotnik Schmidt

Bess's Lament

I didn't know he was a magic man, a shape-shifter. When I met him, he was Erik, trapeze artist, diminutive Jew. I knew he liked strudel, stuffed cabbage, his mother's babka. He held me with his bird fingers—cupping my chin—teasing me with his flashing eyes. I dreamt he was small enough to fit in my pocket. Fold him up in quarters like a white handkerchief, to keep him near.

In the beginning, I was his magic girl. Swish. I hear it still. The whoosh of the black cloth over the box. The swords chiseled in. Never touching my flesh. Stepping out, I smiled. Released from danger. Never scared. Never scarred.

Then he became Houdini. The only trace of our act together, the way he twined and untwined my curls at night. I had my own disappearing act. He dazzled, unlocked manacles, handcuffs, climbed out of milk cans, trunks, coffins. My upside-down man unleashed himself from a straitjacket in midair as I held my breath.

I wanted to always be his gamin girl, to keep a small flame for him, before and even after death. Do ghosts have breath?

In my old age I became what I always was. A forsaken angel with wings of stone

Colleen Geraghty
Grieving Stones

My Mother eats the moon at night
spilling all the butterflies from heaven.
She spits and swears our lives
into a bloodbath of connection.

Eviscerating our future,
her fallen stars,
her ancient longings,
annihilate the light.

She flaunts
her unclaimed hand,
her glutinous embrace,
darkens me

She eats the moon
and in her ruddy mouth
where all her unborn stories
roost

She licks me dry
muzzles my hesitating breath
swallows my innocence
burdens me with her endless brooding gifts
bloody aborted dreams

they sink like grieving stones
into my own sacred heart
obliterating my hopeful eyes
my wishful thinking
all *my* own living dreams

Eileen Howard

Feeding the Fire

"Quisieron enterrarnos, pero se les olvido que somos semillas."
(They tried to bury us, but they didn't know we were seeds.) -A Mexican proverb

Feeding the fire:
slowly.
Building it up
banking it down
feeling it out
making the rounds.

Rants and
chattering.
Silence and
tears.
And
(always)
fears and
fierceness:
balancing
so easily
on an
improbable---impenetrable---trust.

Letting go
loosening up.
Following
the souls of
children
into
mysterious
unknowns---

Letting go
loosening up---

A cyclaminic
act:
turning within
and evoluting
out.

Star-pointed
dandelions,
seeding---
(feeding the fire) and
flinging the
seed on past
ashes anew.

Kappa Waugh

God in the Air

God's presence is like a skunk.
Beautiful in grace she moves
on the dark earth.

Sometimes the faintest trace
reaches you. Nose flares, tests,
tastes the wind. Is she really there?

Then the scent is overwhelming.
How could you ever doubt
the presence of skunk?

Eileen Howard
Epigenetics: Traumatized DNA

Trauma, incarceration, rape, assault:
can these sabotage our own DNA?
Turn genes on and off.
Send rogue chemical markers
marauding through our cellular soup?

Mendel, Darwin, Watson, Crick:
all thought our genetic blueprint
immutable, fixed.
Now comes the murky grey:
something beyond the genome.

Once we argued nature or nurture
around a lively dinner table.
Turns out our lives, our loves, our traumas...
our diets...our mother's diets,
can switch on or switch off genes
in utero and beyond.

How do genes, switched on or off by
experience, pass down to our children?
Our children's children?
Our grandmother eats twinkies, smokes,
votes for Trump: jazzes up our DNA.

Lamarck had a clue.
Something other than Darwin's "natural" selection
hovered in the wings.

Jan Zlotnik Schmidt

Dog Star: Walking My Dog in Logan Park

There is a dog star that watches over them
A dog star
God watches over all of us
A dog star watches over the dogs

The homeless woman in purple
Frayed knit tweed scarves
Around her neck
Her shoelaces untied
Stops and sniffles by a garbage pail

You know this
God loves all his creatures
So he created a dog star
A star to watch over them

She nods waiting for my agreement

I see my dog's paws extended
Floating through space
His eyes taking in
The Milky Way
The aura around the earth

I see his nose sniffing
At blackness at air
Pawing-- a dog paddle
In the celestial dark

Not afraid
Not worrying about
The heat of nebula
Or where his body will land
Just drifting in space,
Lapping up the universe.

She shuffles away,
her shopping cart overflowing
with refuse I can't see except for
the frayed cloth of a comforter.

The torn blue edge of a world.

Eileen Howard

Snow Morph

Snow drifts, drops, dazzles
lightly touches the visible world.
Sneaks under mufflers down boots
Cools, then cools again
the touchable world.

Double tracks meander over
snow covered frozen water
Several stride off
in a determinate diagonal
across to the other side.

Was it a timid deer heading
for sanctuary?
Or a flash of red fox,
his nose locating a
toothsome rabbit on the other shore?

The snow changes our perspective.
With the blur of snow I feel my
own perspective wavering.
There is a grace in this limbo
of swirling change.

Eileen Howard
Similes

THIS is the forest primeval. The murmuring pines and the hemlocks,
Bearded with moss, and in garments green, indistinct in the twilight,
Stand like Druids of eld, with voices sad and prophetic,
Stand like harpers hoar, with beards that rest on their bosoms.
               Henry Wadsworth Longfellow

Half asleep,
pondering similes,
dreamlike, I wonder:
How <u>did</u> druids
of eld stand?
Like portmanteaus
or poltergeists?
Did they fling off their
priestly miens
And run naked as jaybirds?
Little is known of these
ancient Celts, so how did
Longfellow presume to know
their Hemlock stances?
Maybe Henry stood
on the shore of some lake…Imagined these stately, fur clad
serious men
contemplating him
from the opposite shore,
staring back with pinecone eyes,
in dark rain cloud robes.
Henry Wadsworth:
Claiming a poet's prerogative
to pluck similes from the ether,
wind them off a spindle
and weave them into verse.

Jan Zlotnik Schmidt

A Moment Is an Eternity

"A moment is an eternity"
Cesar Manrique
Film: Cesar Manrique Fundacion, Tahiche, Canary Islands)

Sometimes the ocean is indigo and aquamarine.
Sometimes it is tinged blue-grey.

Sometimes the obsidian lava rocks glint in the sun
Sometimes they are ashen or a dull tobacco brown.

Sometimes the breeze brings cool nights
Sometimes there is a hot wind, a calima.

Sometimes the stones, washed by sea foam, glisten.
Sometimes in this dry world they are scarred, rusted brown.

Sometimes the sand hills are layers of pink and terracotta.
Sometimes they are darkened by shadows of clouds.

Sometimes the white stucco houses in the distance dot the hills like wings.
Sometimes they are dwarfed by the vast sky and intense sun.

Sometimes this land of lava fields, volcanic bubbles, camels and desert
seems mummified; sometimes it is alive with ethereal light.

I pick up a stone thrown up by the sea, mottled
by the tides. It is pocked, traces of air still caught inside.

Each moment an eternity.

AGING

Eileen Howard

Ripples in Time

I am looking out my kitchen window.
A young couple travels quickly across the screen.
He pushes a small boy in a black hooded stroller,
his pace brisk. She looks a little strained keeping up.
Gravid with child, gently rounded, her baby bump precedes her.

They are so unfledged! No wrinkles. No wizened brows.
Soon the couple will be reining in the boy,
trying to keep him from flying out of their grasp.
Life moves so fast, there is barely time
for ripples in time's tides.

Older now, my friends and I. My friend carries a cane.
Her husband's walk is stiff and somewhat graceless.
I am a little more mobile, but feel the gravity of age
tugging me by the collar, slowing me down.
How long before there are wakes with no ripples?

Jan Zlotnik Schmidt

Miriam

Miriam went into the desert
Shouted her name into the arc of the wind
shouted her words into rock and desert air
The words of an old woman
who swaddled a child
who knew the creases of infant flesh
the breadth of the child as a man

Miriam sang in the desert
words with timbrel and lyre   with claps of joy
in a world in which the sea divided
and she stepped into an open land
and danced an ecstatic dance with others
their voices peeling off rock crevice and cliffs
and they pressed their weight into the desert

Light danced off the sand
Light twirled into dust and shadow
Darkness shadowed the land
There were voices of rage and dread
The soles of her feet turned white in the desert
turned white until the darkness spilled from her
into an arid land   a wilderness
of her own wandering

Then Miriam in her bent frame and old bones
cast herself into this wilderness
into a land of dreaming and
stretched in the sun's heat and light
Tasted the sun's warmth as manna
as if she were tasting salt of the earth
The land's sorrow and joy lodged in her throat

She lifted her eyes to the heavens
saw the white of the clouds
The blue white translucent sky
The fingers of her right hand cupped the air
She opened her mouth to the heavens
The breadth of the land full in her body
And light spilled from her in words
in a desert of quiet and ceaseless time

This is the way it was in her old age
She swaddled a child by river and reeds
The child came into his own body and breadth
He came into his own greatness
left her body behind
She sang and the sound stemmed her sorrow
She danced in the tumult of her body
clapped her body into being

They marked her place in the desert
with water to remember her body
words and songs and only she knew
the invisible weight of water
The spring and source of words
in the desert of her longing

Colleen Geraghty
Spindrift

It's snowing when I finally leave the nursing home. Big flakes the size of dimes tumble down, melt on my eyelashes, spill like tears. February's great gusts of wind rifle through my hair. I stand in the squalls, breathing winter and hoping the chill cleanses the stink of shit and disinfectant that still clings to me.

Today I'd stayed at the nursing home through supper. I swaddled you in paper towels and shuffled you into the big blue chair. I pushed the supper tray forward and wound your swollen claw-like hand around the big spoon. I lifted the cover from your supper plate and I gagged at the sloppy pallet of pureed peas, creamed beef, mashed potatoes, and applesauce clumped together like throw-up. More odors piled around the stench of shit, piss, and disinfectant. I look into your vacant eyes. I grab your wrist in my hand. "Eat it slowly or you'll choke," I command.

"Choke, choke," you echo. Your shaky hand plunges the big spoon into the sloppy mounds. Without pausing, you shovel, shovel, gulp, gulp.

"Slow down," I command, grabbing your wrist, trying to modulate the spoon's up and down. I guide it slowly to your lips and, when you have the rhythm, I release your wrist. I stand at your side watching you plunge into the mess, big spoon circling round and round, scooping and scraping the plate. You shovel lump after leaky lump into your mouth, your tongue thrusting in and out like a birdie from a cuckoo clock. Peas slide down your chin, thick green sludge congeals in the wrinkles on your neck. One hefty spoonful misses your mouth and plops between your thighs.

"I'm wet," you shout, but keep shoveling. Pureed beef slides down your wrist, plops between your breasts and soaks through the paper towels.

Gurgle, gurgle, fart, fart, shovel, shovel and then one loud wet toot from your behind. "I shit," you shout.

"Ok, let's use the commode."

"No, supper, supper. I want supper."

I'm too exhausted to argue with you. The heat's turned up so high on the Dementia Unit today that moisture drips down every window and pools under the radiators. I yawn and decide to let you sit in your shitty diaper, your spoon circling the plate -- shovel, shovel, gulp, gulp.

You wiggle forward in the blue chair, a diaper full of crap leaking through your lilac pants, green sludge staining your neck, mashed potatoes squished between your thighs, and pureed beef soiling your blouse. I sit across from you and wrap my winter scarf around my mouth to keep from gagging. You pick up the plate and lick it clean. Fingers sticky, you drop the plate onto the tray and shout, "Ice cream, ice cream."

I open the little cup of ice cream, spoon it into your mouth. You smile, grin, bare your teeth, clap your sticky hands in the air and shout again, "Ice cream, ice cream."

You lurch for the cup but I hold on tight. I spoon creamy white clumps onto your tongue.

"More, more," you gulp. Spoon after spoon, I scrape the bottom of the Styrofoam cup, give you the last spoonful, and turn the cup upside down. "Look, all gone," I tell you, handing you the empty cup. "How about some juice? I ask."

"Juice, juice, red juice!"

I remove the lid from the bright red juice and hold it to your lips. "Slow, slow, take it slow." But you're nothing but big gulps today and suddenly you're choking. Beet red face, tears streaming down your cheeks. I pound you on the back and you gurgle, "More, more."

When you stop choking, I offer you another sip, but this time you spit juice all over your tray, a fine spray of red spatters my lap like pinpricks of blood.

We're a sticky, stinking mess today but at least you've eaten your supper.

I wipe, wash, scrub, and then I change your diaper because I know the unit is short staffed. I remove your soiled clothes and pull your nightgown over your head. I settle you into your bed. Your eyelids sag shut. We're both weary.

You've had a bad couple of days. The nurses told me that you've been pulling your hair out, big fistfuls of white and remnants of Clairol red. Yesterday, after you'd ripped your bangs until you bled, the charge nurse shaved your forehead. You've bitten yourself again too. Big ugly scabs dot your wrists. You pick the scabs, try to bite them, but I pull your arms away and shout, "No, no, we don't eat scabs."

You lurch for my earrings and yank. "Mine, mine," you shout.

"No, they're mine," I tell you, pushing your hands away.

You frown, grab the hair behind your ears, yank fistfuls, and throw wisps of white into the air.

"No, don't pull your hair," I groan. I sit now on edge of the bed. "Here, have a pillow."

We play peek-a-boo and you lift your arms and cover your face, again and again. "Peek-a-boo, I see you. Peek-a-boo, I see you."

But do you see me?

Your eyes are glazed and cloudy as a frozen day. Yellow crud rests in the corners where tears used to flow. I sit beside you on the bed while outside, the hag of winter throws a wailing tantrum, flings snow and ice against the window panes. In dementia's paradise, it's murky as hell and I'm surrounded by wizened old men, crippled women, wheelchairs, walkers, hoists, bedpans, urinals, diapers, pureed food, and the stench of shit and piss.

I mouth breathe. I get up and go to the sink, let the water run. I scrub and scrub the gooey spots off my hands, my arms, and, while the water's running, I remember last night's dream:

We were standing at the shore, you and me, ankle deep in spindrift, the ocean roaring and lapping at our legs. You are wrinkled and old, your brain porous as cheesecloth, your head wobbling in the breeze like a bobble doll. I've got you tied to me by a length of rope. Around my waist, anchored up near my heart, an umbilicus of caring binds us like a boat tied tight to her mooring.

You are half-in, half-out, half-witted in the water. I hold the length of rope, it pulses wet in my hand, slackens, and I usher you out into deeper waters. In these waves, you're not screaming obscenities at nurses, you're not gulping and choking on pureed beef, you're not mewing like a cat, pulling your hair out, spitting juice, lurching for my earrings, or biting your own arm. In this bright water dream we are quietly witnessing the horizon line. We are shuffling out into deeper waters. As the ocean chants her salty tune and seaweed snakes around our ankles, the seagulls and shore birds are circling above, witnessing the length of rope that's bound you to fifty years of suffering. I am ushering you deeper into the sea. I'm rolling you over onto

your back, my hands lifting and supporting you as I slowly let out lengths of rope and watch you float. Knee deep, thigh deep, waist deep in the water, my feet dig into the sand below and I whisper, "Float, float, that's right, float."

Silly prayers uttered to the gods of water. I am praying for the ocean's roar, for that mighty wave, for the great heave-ho of the undertow to pull taut the rope and finally break this umbilicus of caring.

Snap, snap, one quick rupture and there you would go, floating, floating out into the waves.

Jan Zlotnik Schmidt

I Am Your Dutiful Daughter

I am your dutiful daughter
These words are carved on my flesh

I will wash crusted sleepers
From your eyes
Clip the whiskers
On your chin
Cool your skin
With rose water
In summer's heat

I will enter
The dark swamp
Of your unwashed dreams
Pull your neck
Shoulders torso toes
From the muck

I will preserve
Your quiet
Like peaches preserved
Glistening in a jar
And smooth
Out the wrinkles of
Knowing and unknowing
At your behest

And as your eyes
Glaze into forgetfulness
I will settle next
To your bones
Your breath
Your empty breasts
As your secrets
Spill from my dreams

Eileen Howard
The Wasp

Consigned to a life of
perpetual banishment,
the lonely wasp
finally flew in
the open window
and crisipated himself
on my naked light bulb.
As fleeting as the smoke of
summer,
he wafted in,
crinkled before our eyes,
and was no more...
A puff---a slight buzzing
of engaging mortality,
then gone.

Jan Zlotnik Schmidt

Cross at the Beach

Her fingers grazed a mound of sand. Cool damp prickles like stings under the flat of her palms.

She remembers it that way. Kneeling, on a cold windy day in winter, her hands brushing over the contours of the mound, the size of an upside down baby's cradle. Her father too staring down at the curious site in the sand.

Then they both were startled to see a cross of twigs, thin saplings strapped together with a rubber band, perched at the end of the hillock. Her fingers traced the outlines of the cross in air, not wanting to touch it, to disturb the site. Her father stood next to her, both of them, absorbed in the mystery of the moment.

They had come to the deserted beach, to the ocean in Rockaway, as they often did on cold winter Sunday mornings when she was a teenager, he to scavenge for gnarled scraps of driftwood, she to find the purple iridescent insides of mussel shells thrown up by the waves. Usually they took off on their own—to return a bit later and compare their finds. That day she wandered off, and as she returned to their meeting place, saw the mound ahead of her. At first she thought it was just a ridge of sand on the rutted beach. When she got closer, she saw the unmistakable proportions of a grave or a burial mound. He traveled from the other end of the beach to meet her at the spot.

She stared, then bent down, brushed her

fingers over the top of the mound, trying to figure out what it was. He silently watched her. Was it a child's devilish prank? Was it the grave of a beloved pet, bird, cat or dog? Or was there nothing buried there—just stones and shells caught in the sand. Was the ridge just a peculiar formation of a winter sea?

She sees the scene now in memory—the blue gray sky, the white line of the horizon, the cross gaining gargantuan proportions—large against clouds and blue gray ocean—like a Georgia O'Keefe painting of an animal skull or bones against desert and a vast blue sky. For a time they didn't talk, didn't poke a finger or stick into the mound to figure out what was there. Perhaps they were afraid of what they'd find. Instead quietly they looked down and after a few minutes left the beach.

When she asks him in his old age if he recalls that day, that scene, their time together, with eyes barely lit by knowledge or desire, he tells her he doesn't remember anything.

Her fingers graze a house of sand. His lips touch air. She hears the stifled murmurs of his heart. Quiet almost still.

Perhaps buried in that grave is only a stone. Milky white sea glass. Dense in the center, open to the sun at the edges, light sifting through when she holds it against the sky.

Mary K O'Melveny

Emergency Room Redux

We are waiting in dim light
in a near-empty hospital hallway.
It is well past midnight.
My mother is angry, tired of all the ways
that fear arrives, not quite
sure if her wildly beating heart
is simply nearing its end of days,
about to fail outright,
or if some lesser malaise
is causing her to fall apart.

I am tired as well, fearful too.
I wanted her to stay vibrant, clear
of thought, as she once was -- a debut
not an exit. This is not our first time here
in this basement awaiting tests,
vital sign reports. We have viewed
many results of ER doctors' requests.
She moves slowly by gurney, disappears
for scans she has often passed through
without a backward glance or protest.

As we struggle to keep awake
in the emergency room's near-silence,
we avoid exchanges that on another
day might bond us, such give and take
easier on a sunlit porch. Here, science
is our only muse. As we wait together
to discuss medical news, we cannot fake
our disappointments. We are compliant
as daybreak dawns. Since I would rather
be anywhere else, I stay quiet for my sake.

Finally, all poking and prodding is done,
fluids checked, electrolytes measured,
x-rays surveyed. A doctor – a new one –
steps into our curtained space. He has heard
we have been here all night. He sports a smile.
The news is good, he says – *You can go back home.*
He does not see that my mother was tethered
to the waiting. Soon enough, he steps back to the aisle,
moves on to others, checking new ledgers.
She stares ahead, eyes moist, toward a new day. Alone.

Tana Miller

Drought

sweet cherry season ends
two weeks early   Lake Ontario
recedes from its shore   flaunts
cracked mud wrinkles   brackish puddles
a heron stands on one thin leg   surveys
the leaves hanging   wilted   lifeless
from the trees that line the shore
even the frogs are still
dust-to-dust the crisp brown weeds
whisper into the hot air
dust-to-dust

mother   bald   still beautiful
lies in the narrow white bed
brain   breasts   lungs invaded   green eyes
almost sightless   flash
fury   terror   as she
endures her final July draught

Kit Goldbaugh
Ethel

All five of Tuesday's volunteers are in the sorting room of the church thrift shop today. There were several donations over the weekend, and Ethel reminds everyone that many hands make light work. Ethel is chatty today. Her physical must have gone well, thinks Rosie. Ethel tells everyone that at this recent annual physical, her doctor had asked her if she wore children's clothing. Ethel is 92 years old and 92 pounds heavy. She says, "It isn't like I was wearing shirts with peace signs."

"Or 'juicy' on the butt," offers Rosie, assisting Ethel to her chair. She moves the stuffed gorilla to the floor and frees the chair for Ethel. "Watch out for the whoopee cushion," she says to Ethel and gets back to unpacking donations.

Taylor, the new college student volunteer smiles while holding her finger in place for Ethel to tag a set of candlesticks oh so slowly.

"What did you say, Ethel?" asks Taylor.

"Me?" says Ethel. "What did I say to who?"

"To your doctor, Ethel," calls Doris from the back. "What did you say to your doctor when he asked if you wear children's clothing?"

"I said not on purpose."

Louise smiles. "Maybe you should wear more provocative clothing the next time you see him, Ethel." Then, "Oh, there is my apron," she says and undresses the huge stuffed gorilla now sitting next to Ethel. Louise continues, "Sometimes people donate adult lingerie. Let us dress you for your next doctor's appointment. Nobody will ask if you are wearing children's clothing when we finish your make-over, Ethel."

"I'm pretty good with make-up," offers Taylor.

"Ethel, when is your next appointment?" asks Doris from behind a stack of boxes.

But Ethel isn't listening. "Does anyone know why Magilla is always sitting in my chair when we get here?" she asks, genuinely puzzled. "Do you owe anybody money?" asks Rosie.

Just then, Mrs. Moskowitz from the high school drama club calls into the sorting room, "Greetings, everyone. As expected, I've found great treasures. You never disappoint, and I'd like to check out when one of you nice ladies has a minute."

"Hello, Doris. Hello Ethel. Ethel, I hope I'll see you at our first play this year."

"If I'm still alive and haven't broken a hip," replies Ethel very softly, almost whispering to the lampshade she is pricing. She smiles at Taylor.

"Okay, Mrs. Moskowitz," smiles Louise and ushers her to the checkout table. "And how are preparations for this year's play?"

Back in the sorting room, Ethel asks

Taylor if she knows what play they are doing this year. "It is one of those sad ones again? Last year was one of the sad ones. *Death of a Mockingbird* I think."

That sounds about right thinks Rosie.

Louise returns with a shoe-box full of tiny glass figurines. Each is carefully wrapped in tissue. There is a green frog with gemstones embedded on his back and tiny emerald eyes. There is an orange goldfish with delicate white fins, and an amber horse head.

"Wow. They are so pretty."

Doris climbs over the boxes to see. "They are really pretty but what do people do with this stuff?" Taylor wonders aloud. "Maybe they are from *The Glass Menagerie*," says Rosie. "That was it!" says Ethel.

The glass animals are lovely, everyone agrees. Louise answers, "Well, I'm not certain that people do much of anything with them except to display them. They're just pretty." "Oh, Ethel," Louise turns to Ethel." Mrs. Moskowitz says she hopes that you'll come to the play this year." "Oh, I don't know. I don't like those sad stories. I like musicals, but maybe I will go with the seniors on the bus," says Ethel. "What do you think, Rosie?"

Rosie doesn't hear the question. She is examining the glass menagerie. First, she picks up the glass fish. Possibly, it was hand blown. It has tiny green gemstone eyes. Never taking her own eyes off the fish, she says, "Let's say you were playing *The Godfather*." Doris navigates to the table.

Rosie tears off a piece of newspaper and wraps the fish in it. Then she and the fish leave the room. A minute later they return with a bridegroom doll holding the paper wrapped fish. The groom doll hands the fish to the toy gorilla, now sitting in a director's chair by the coats. Rosie quotes, "'Luca Brasi sleeps with the fishes,'"

Nobody says anything, but Louise is smiling.

Next, Rosie takes the groom doll again and tucks it into a makeshift bed on the sorting table. She slips the glass horse next to the doll's feet. She looks up and says, "Let's say you get to the part of the story where Jack Woltz has been given an offer that he can't refuse." She lays the groom doll in the toy bed and places the wrapped glass horse at his feet and then covers both with a dish towel blanket. Rosie smiles. "I suppose with enough cardboard boxes and tempera paint, you could even build a tiny movie set."

Ethel asks, "Why do you want to play *Godfather*?" The sorting room is quiet for a few seconds. Taylor looks to Louise. Louise to Rosie. "Oh, I don't want to play *Godfather*," Rosie responds. "The question was, 'what are these for?' I was suggesting possible uses for these glass animals beyond their decorative beauty."

Louise clears her throat. *"The Glass Menagerie."*

"That's it!" says Ethel, surprised again. "That was the play." So not *Death of a Mockingbird* then, thinks Rosie. She says to Ethel, "That was a sad story." "Yes," agrees Ethel. "I think it was Tennessee Ernie Ford. I remember the glass animals and the shy girl," she continues, "I do get things mixed up, though. Was *The Godfather* the one with Spencer Tracy?"

"Tennessee Williams wrote *The Glass Menagerie.* And it was Brando, not Spencer Tracy" says Rosie stuffing her cheeks with tissues and donning a fedora. "Ethel my goddaughter, I will grant you any wish on this my daughter's wedding day."

"Speaking of weddings, don't you have a wedding coming up soon, Ethel? Your grandson in Florida?" asks Louise.

"In two weeks."

"Are you staying for a while?" calls Doris.

"I'm staying with my daughter and her husband for two weeks."

"Oh, Ethel! Can we help pick out your clothes for the trip?"

Ethel looks at her feet and the pants falling over her shoes. "These pants did used to be too short for me," she says and then, looking up, "I do need to dress for Florida weather."

And so over the next two weeks, the thrift shop volunteers select a wardrobe of brand new gently used summer clothes and accessories for Ethel's adventure. The day before her flight, Taylor manicures her ancient arthritic hands.

"Do you like to fly?" asks Taylor, brushing on the second coat of *Avon Beat Breast Cancer Pink* polish, a donation.

"I don't mind. They used to serve drinks and meals. Peanuts. Now I just want an aisle seat." She looks at her hands. This looks so pretty! Thank you, Theresa."

"It was my pleasure, Ethel. It's Taylor,

not Theresa."

"Taylor. Taylor. Taylor. I've seen you hang clothes like a tailor. Taylor." Ethel shakes her head. "You did really nice work on my hands. Thank you."

"It really was my pleasure, Ethel. I enjoyed our visit."

Ethel's daughter Linda walks in the shop. She bears a Dolly- the- sheep resemblance to her mother. "Ready, Mom?" she calls in Ethel's voice. "We're off to the airport in Albany, and then to Florida."

"We'll see you in two weeks. Have fun, Ethel." The staff walks Ethel to the car.

"Oh, Ethel. I won't see you for even longer than that," says Rosie. " I'm going to Colorado to see my son next week. We'll swap stories when you get back"

The group walks to the car with Ethel.

"Godspeed, Ethel."

A few weeks later, Rosie returns to the shop. In Colorado, she had attended a memorial for her daughter-in-law. At the one-year anniversary, the family unveiled her gravestone. No one in the shop knew the reason for her trip. Rosie is gratefully returning to the comfortable monotony of folding clothes or tagging kitchen magnets. "Hey. Has anyone heard from Ethel? She must be back by now."

Silence follows and then, Lucy speaks up.

"Ethel died. You weren't here."

"Neither was Ethel," says Doris.

"What? When? What happened?"

"She was in Florida. For the wedding.

The grandson's, Joe. Well, she got to the wedding and all, but about a week later, the other grandson committed suicide. Can you imagine? Ethel died after his funeral. Not the one who got married, Joe, but Frankie. The one with the curly hair. Linda's boy. Drugs."

"Oh my God," whispers Rosie. "Oh my God. That's so awful. That's so sad."

"Yeah," agrees Lucy. "She was my friend, you know. We went bowling together."

The whole time that Lucy is talking, she is unconsciously dressing the gorilla in Ethel's apron. "There's going to be a service here next Saturday. They can't bury her though. The ground's too wet. She'd keep coming up.

Rosie wills Lucy to stop talking about the soggy ground and the coffin, but Lucy continues on and on, telling everyone that the same thing happened with her poor Charlie and they had to wait until very late spring for his burial. This is a big problem in New Orleans, too, continues Lucy.

"Ewee," blurts Taylor involuntarily.

"Oh, it's a real problem, the weather," continues Lucy.

"We had a cat we kept in the freezer until spring." With that, Rosie slips into the linens section. One shelf at a time, she empties linens into a basket and refolds towels and sheets and blankets. She snaps the towels and pillowcases. She folds and creases fitted sheets into squares and bundles sheet sets and towels and ties a ribbon on each bundle.

Later that day, Ethel's daughter Linda enters the shop with a box of clothes.

Hers is the shipwrecked face of grief. Louise hands the box to Doris, embraces Linda, and together they walk to her car and back with boxes of Ethel's worldly goods.

In the sorting room, Rosie lays a stack of Ethel's clothes on the table for sorting: KEEP, PLANET AID and TRASH.

"Ethel was funny," said Lucy. "You should of known her." Behind the table, she pets each item from Ethel's box. "Me and Ethel were on the same bowling team. The Pin-Curls we called ourselves." She sighs or catches her breath, Rosie can't tell because Lucy keeps talking. "This was her bowling jacket. She was funny, too. When she put stuff in the PLANET AID bin, she said that she imagined those Shamrock Run shirts on refugees."

Rosie remembered that event differently. It was Luke and Tiffany's Wedding, not the Shamrock Run. Ethel had folded a stack of T-shirts proclaiming *I survived Luke and Tiffany's Wedding 6/25/2004* "Can you imagine a refugee camp of Sudanese in these foolish shirts? I'm over 90 and I still don't get God's sense of humor."

So not funny ha-ha or peculiar, but funny ironic and insightful, thought Rosie.

Lucille and Doris examined Ethel's sweaters for pins, pockets for pennies, pants for pee stains. The last they did discreetly, whispering about Ethel's little problem and discarding virtually all of Ethel's slacks. Rosie observed, glad that Ethel was being treated respectfully, and thinking then, only a hobbit could have worn them anyway. Rosie thought Ethel might smile at that.

"We can't sell this," declares Lucy of Ethel's Pin Curls jacket. And so, ever so gently, Rosie and Lucy dress Magilla in Ethel's monogrammed bowling jacket and thrift shop staff apron. They do it with a kind of reverence. Rosie sits Magilla on high chair that will never see the main floor.

For the next hour, the group unpacks the rest of Ethel's things. Her daughter had said that she wanted everyone to please take a keepsake. Ethel had loved this church. She loved this shop.

Ethel had long ago given away her jewelry, china, silver. There was some costume jewelry, gloves, paperweights. Rosie picked up Ethel's well-worn cookbook. Several pages were marked with notations or post-its. One post-it read *Be still and know that I am God* in Ethel's penmanship. "I'd like Ethel's cookbook," said Rosie.

Jan Zlotnik Schmidt

If I think of My Life

My life in my twenties
a clean white space
an unwritten page
Now the lines
are drawn, the ink splattered
The curves of letters not visible,
just blossoming patches of dead petals
pressed in the book

forties an open field
The grasses now flattened
the reeds rusted
the milkweed pods open bruised
dried   white clouds
still sticking to empty shells

now at sixty
I see the faint blue
of a Giotto sky
And starlings hovering
in the upper most reaches of bare trees
Occasionally
one flies alone
while the others gather
pitch into the blue

How quiet it is   how still
when almost nothing stirs

Colleen Geraghty
Fraudulent Objects

Note to younger self:

A ham sandwich seems an ordinary after Easter Monday lunch
but your mayonnaise mouth purples
when he chokes the pig out of you
for taking too much—
Him teaching you, and the rest of us, still sitting stunned at the table—
it takes a pig to know a pig—
Him showing us what happens when gluttonous hands take
more than they're worth.

What a surprise then
when your second-grade teacher offered you a violin!
Out of the ordinary, she said, you possessed the rarest of gifts, perfect pitch.
She didn't know a rosined bow could blister flesh red,
scar lips, muzzle the music, mute the song.
Him teaching you not to put on airs,
not to raise an uppity racket, disturb his sleep.

How many pages of newspaper did you have to eat?
Wad after thick wad
of shredded comics or sports pages or Ann Landers' advice columns,
even Snoopy congealing in your throat.
Your wallpapered gullet sticky with ordinary words,
empty crossword puzzles—
Him teaching you to remember that in his goddamn house
he wanted his newspaper brought inside before it rained.

How many ordinary pots of leftover beef-and-potato stews
would he smother with liquid soap, scoop into bowls in hefty portions,
commanding you to eat it? Sudsy mouthful after sudsy mouthful
lathering your throat until the sun rose yellow in a milky sky,
shit bursting bubbles down your skinny legs—
all this because you'd forgotten again
to wash the stew pot before you went to bed?

Two-faced, double-crossing, fraudulent pigs, these ordinary objects,
clandestine weapons, hidden even in a basket of eggs
broken into your hair so you'd remember
he wanted his eggs over-easy,
so you'd finally absorb his rule of thumb,
memorize his canon, learn to march
to the beat of his hard-hitting, law-and-order drum.

Even holy gifts, like your First Communion rosary,
moon-white, little heaven pearls, tied to a sterling crucifix,
given after you'd received the Body of Christ,
crushed under the heel of his boot, ground to a fine dust
because you'd failed again
to memorize the Act of Contrition.

When you come of age in a house bullied
by ordinary objects,
where an after Easter Monday ham can suffocate you senseless,
news can perish in your gullet like banished books and unread stories,
where a violin's bow can scorch tender flesh, and you,
slick with the soapy shit stew of life boiling in your belly,
you witness God, crushed, ground to dust under the heel of an angry boot,
inside a house he calls a home.

You know every ordinary object, on any ordinary day,
becomes a weapon.

Is it any wonder you feel hollow as a broken little bone,
wake-up glass-fragile,
always have cold feet?

Mary K O'Melveny

Notes from a Tehran Marketplace

Tell them I want to have
a normal life said Amir
as he stood by his stall
selling zippo lighters
and water pipes that glistened
in the afternoon sun.

Can you find my daughter
a job? asked Nasrin as
she adjusted her head scarf
and declined to give her
last name in case her words
might suggest some offense.

Two elderly women
climb down from a pink bus
on Sadeghiyeh Square,
clutching their shopping bags
as if they might contain
gold coins, not tangerines.

A young woman plays Adele
on her keyboard, as her
brother croons beside her,
his wheelchair swaying to
the rhythm. His baseball
cap says *Boston Red Sox.*

Shadi, a young woman
stood at the veil seller's
as she wondered aloud
whether to protest again
or just speak Bach's language
to her piano students.

Mr. Faraji did not bother
to listen to the newscasts.
His perfume shop opened
when the nuclear deal
was signed. He imagined
scents of narcissus, musk

and ambergris filling
the air, how his wares would
soften the skin of hopeful
ladies and aromas of victory
would fill the air like crowns
of myrtle and myrrh bestowed

on ancient infantries,
where roadsides were filled with
smoke of aloe, rosewater
celebrated martial triumphs.
Now, his stall is shuttered as
the fragrance of peace drifts away.

This poem was inspired by an article in the
New York Times on Friday, May 11, 2018
by reporter Thomas Erdbrink exploring
reactions of Iranians in Tehran's Sadeghiyah
Square marketplace to the United States'
withdrawal from the Iranian nuclear accord
(the JCPOA).

Mary K O'Melveny

Have You Seen... *An American Story*

I.

Have you seen my son Jesus cries a young
mother from behind barred walls, concrete
rising behind her like an icy curtain
even though it offers no cool shelter
from dank Texas air. Even her tears run
hot on her face. *He is only seven*
she wails to anyone who would listen.
But she is surrounded by other mourners
whose sounds cannot be silenced. Weeping
echoes down corridors but yields no answers.

Each woe-filled woman clutches some totem as if
it could call her child back to her: baby blue
sunglasses, a broken plastic watch,
a smudged shirt, a torn hair ribbon that once
held a daughter's braids when their caravan
began many months back. *When will someone
tell me where Rosa has been taken? Please?*
The dour faced guards show no emotion,
their eyes impenetrable even as the mothers'
weather-beaten faces close in before them.

No one needs to translate anguish in these
steel rimmed chambers and no one in charge
cares to do so. Sometimes, when a buzzer
skins the air to announce a visitor,
sobbing subsides briefly, as if each
detainee could will the guard toward her,
to walk her to the immigration lawyers
or social workers who know things she does not.
Too soon, optimism slips away,
dissolving like a late day desert mist.

II.

Have you seen Running Deer? My son's new school
has lost him. They say he is now Robert.
A minister stands at the church school door,
holding a cane made of birch. His eyes
are hollow, his mouth is set. *Your son ran*
away. He says this in a voice so loud
it hurts my ears. As if I could not follow
his meaning unless he shouted like wind.
They forced me to bring my son here. Told me
he would learn how to be *American.*

Preachers, teachers, soldiers promised he would
learn *useful* skills, improve his circumstances.
When he spoke their language, prayed to a *real*
God, his chances to thrive would have no limits.
We had no choice, of course. They lined up our
children at the railway station and marched
them away. We wrestled with our tears as
if they were the cougars hunting our young.
Pale Hawk, Dancing Rabbit each took my boy's
hands so he would not turn toward our grief.

Now gone, no one will help me recover him.
No one knows a *Robert* from a *Peter*
or a *Daniel.* Forced from home, shamed,
shunned, proud histories stolen, tribal tales
forbidden, our children vanished before
we could blink, slipped into night without a
look back, footfalls soft as a piñon branch.
Some died. Others were recaptured, beaten,
sent off to wars. I still wait for star
spirit guides to escort him back to me.

III.

Amanda's scream pierces the air as if
a hatchet had been wielded against the walls.
Please don't take my baby from me she howls,
refusing to give up her newborn even
as the lash stripes her back. Some auction block
bidders seem discomfited by such noise.
A few turn away in dismay but most
look on impatiently. Soon enough,
her son is forcibly removed. Her blood-stained
arms flail like windmills. She is sold, dragged off.

Years later, Amanda will place a notice
in a local newspaper. *Have you seen my boy?*
He was sold in 1851 to Roger Fuller
of Walker County. I lived on the farm
of Benjamin Major until my freedom. Please
do me the Great Favor of helping me find my
child. She will place these notices as often
as she can, as long as she lives. She believes,
in her deep heart, that god will reunite them,
that she will know her son's voice when he speaks.

At war's end, advertisements sprouted like
fertile crops, seeded with names of missing
children, husbands, wives, parents, siblings.
Maps, dates of sales and re-sales, owner
lists, likely places of transfer and terror.
All gleaned from memory's dimming light.
Have you seen... Last seen...Once seen....
*Information wanted...*Each word winds like a
thick vine around a heart. Each sorrow is reborn.
Each limb still aches from the tearing away.

Tana Miller

Jump Jim Crow

Leeds, Alabama 1953

one summer evening we drove to the high school football field
a family outing   mama daddy granny granddaddy my little sisters
we strolled around the field
stopped to chat with cousin Violet Lou
breathed her lily of the valley and face powder smell
as she hugged us one-by-one
at dusk we found seats in the bleachers
a pigeon-breasted woman sang under a flower-bedecked arbor
the air cooled   the earth held its breath
klansmen   dressed in long white robes   masks   tall pointed hats
poured onto the field   paraded around and around
burned a giant wooden cross
everyone cheered   I clapped and clapped
the next day I asked granny for old sheets   my sisters and I
played KKK under the black walnut tree all afternoon

Rosendale, New York 2018

in the deep night   wracked by the racial injustice
that threatens to snap our country asunder
I am haunted by thoughts of people my family owned
by the nights they rode out on country roads in white hoods
by the heavy nooses they strung in trees
by the black people they forced off sidewalks as they strolled along
I ask   over-and-over   how can I say I am sorry

Colleen Geraghty
Every Soft Thing

Some things in life come to you hard, pulling you into yourself like a house into the fist of a hurricane. And other stuff comes up on you real slow, tip-toed and soft, and before you know it, you're bruised as old fruit and wishing you'd been born dead, as dead as one of Aunt Margie's babies.

Everybody was always talking and whispering about them babies on the hush-hush. Seemed Aunt Margie had nothing but worthless problem babies that brung her to her knees. She was always bent-backed and crying, running to the bathroom and spilling herself all over everything. She prayed at the altar for hours on end, spent dime after dime on holy candles and never left us a cent for penny candy and still she never got it right. Problem babies was all she ever had.

Once or twice she got some old doctor named McDonald to sew a stitch way up in her privates, just to keep her from slipping a baby, to keep her from leaving a mess on the stairs, in her underwear, and Christ Almighty, one time, all over the street by the fire house in the middle of the Fourth of July Parade. There weren't no Mummers to speak of in July parades but everybody in Philly loved the Fourth anyway. The marching band was always good and them baton twirlers threw up so high, they stunned us. Everybody loved the razzle-dazzle of the Fourth but then Aunt Margie went

to slipping a damn baby, a bloody damn mess all over the concrete, wrecking the whole sparkling day.

"McDonald stitch or no McDonald stitch," my big sister complained. "Aunt Margie's babies won't take hold even if Uncle Jimmy punches her worthless baby-slipping ass to Timbuktu and back. She already gave him three girls, but la-dee-da, he wants another boy."

"But he's already got a boy," my little sister said. "He's got Peter."

"He don't want some skinny-assed, scrawny-legged, milky-white, bloodshot boy," my sister hollered. "He wants a REAL boy."

"He is a real boy, isn't he?"

"You call that pansy-ass a boy? My brother asked. "There ain't no belt wide enough to cure that sissy."

"You're one to talk," my big sister said, "Why'da'ya think we ended up with another baby brother, huh? Aunt Margie's gotta keep trying till she gets it right."

Everybody in Philly, even Father Finnegan, wanted Aunt Margie to shape up and get a hold of herself. But no sir, she just couldn't do it. No matter how many times she went to confession or how many headstands she did up the cellar wall when she shoulda been down there loading the washer, she just kept making a mess of things.

Some things in life just come to you hard and some things tiptoe softy behind you and before you even feel God's breath on your neck, you're melting, you're lost and you're disappointing everybody. Life's slippery that way, one minute you think you gotta hold of it and the next minute it's worse than soap. Just getting used to the hard when the soft comes along and slips it to you good and you can't get up off your knees, two round circles of red, burnt to a crisp from kneeling and praying, genuflecting, and begging Christ Almighty for some damn miracle to put an end to your slippery suffering. Poor Aunt Margie, she was a mess of a mess, kneeling and praying, taking the hard, the soft and everything in between.

Mrs. Feeney from down the street felt so terrible for Aunt Margie, she gave her a bottle of her St. Bernadette water and three damn holy cards of St. Brigid. Everybody over at the parish knew that poor Brigid had it tough in her day too.

"But for God's sakes," my sister said, "Take look at that bitch now. Pope Paul the 100th, or whatever his name was, shot Brigid outa the holy cannon, sent her ass all the way to Heaven."

"Yeah, and before that bitch even knew what hit her," cousin Katie exclaimed, "She was wearing a crown of light, some midnight mascara and one heck of a lot of rouge. Take a look at her statue the next time you're over near the convent."

"The one where she looks kinda like Liz Taylor only she's dressed like a nun?"

"That's the one. God don't want his lady saints dressed like movie stars when he's gotta have all the attention on himself."

"There ain't no movie stars at Heaven's gate, stupid. They get the escalator down, if you know what I mean."

I'd seen St. Brigid hiding in her grotto over at the convent, wondered if her mother had ever taught that bitch to clean her ears 'cause she sure wasn't listening to Aunt Margie. After all Pope Paul did for St. Brigid, adorning her with Easter lilies, plastering her face on a million holy cards, throwing her a feast day and a novena so she could cure every disease known to women, I thought St. Brigid oughta toss Aunt Margie a miracle or two. After all the dimes Aunt Margie spent buttering that bitch up with prayers, St. Brigid owed Aunt Margie a million miracles, or at least she shoulda found it in her heart to keep Aunt Margie from slipping the next babe.

The whole damn neighborhood had missed out on the fireworks on account of Aunt Margie and her mess but you'd never have known it from watching Mrs. Feeney and those Rosary bitches. One Sunday after mass, they circled around Aunt Margie, stroking and patting and hush-hush whispering at her like she was a half-dead kitten. While Mrs. Feeney rubbed St. Bernadette water all over Aunt Margie, Mrs. Reilly hung a St. Brigid medal on a string around her neck where it hung low, next to her heart.

Aunt Margie stood there crying and carrying on, melting like a candle at a baptismal. She thanked them for their prayers and then held up her best cake on the fancy plate she kept for Communions and wakes and she smiled into the hope that those Rosary bitches might finally forgive her for the mess she'd made of the Fourth of July.

While they ate her best cake and bit into the memory of her wrecking their one sparkling parade of a day, Aunt Margie hung onto the prayer that a couple of sprinkles of Bernadette water, one goddamn Brigid medal and a little pineapple-upside-down cake might help her get it right this time.

When the pat-pat, cake-talk, feel-sorry-for-Aunt-Margie-party was finally over, them rosary bitches smiled and congratulated her on the new rise of her round belly. They rubbed her back, kissed her on the forehead, and told her they'd say novenas for her.

"Maybe after all that great cake Aunt Margie might finally hold onto something for a change," my sister whispered.

But some things in life, I guess, aren't meant for keeping. A few months later, Aunt Margie slipped another mess all over her new bathroom rug. The hard and the soft just took to Aunt Margie. When one of her slippery babies hit the hard of the street or fell like bruised fruit into the toilet or ran down her legs like they couldn't stand the sight of nothing but God, Aunt Margie shriveled up worse than Uncle Billy, who was home from the war, but still smelt the whole dead mess in the meat of his palms.

Poor Aunt Margie and her slippery babies, for all her trying and praying to St. Brigid, she just couldn't get it right, every soft thing just coming to her hard.

Mary K O'Melveny

The Sounds of Truth Vanishing

In the end, truth vanished too quietly.
There was a certain wonder to it all.
We stared out at distant specks of light
as though we had drifted into space.

There was a certain wonder to it all
as we imagined it still flickering,
as though we had drifted into space,
while once familiar places faded away.

As we imagined it still flickering
like echoes of a gentle chorale,
while once familiar places faded away,
we struggled to recall the journey.

Like echoes of a gentle chorale,
we began to keep tiny secrets.
We struggled to recall the journey,
starting with small adornments to our own histories.

We began to keep tiny secrets
long before P.T. Barnum stepped onstage,
starting with small adornments to our own histories
as if crocheting rubies onto a hangman's rope.

Long before P.T. Barnum stepped onstage,
we tried to add hints of hopeful sparkle,
as if crocheting rubies onto a hangman's rope,
mournful ends traded for cheery platitudes.

We tried to add hints of hopeful sparkle,
discarding facts like childish thoughts,
mournful ends traded for cheery platitudes.
Soon we could only hear what pleased us.

Discarding facts like childish thoughts,
we chose nicer words to match new visions.
Soon we could hear only what pleased us
as the known world slipped away.

We chose nicer words to match new visions.
Amazed at how far we had traveled
as the known world slipped away,
we sometimes said *Remember when* ....

Amazed at how far we had traveled,
we met those who did not understand why
we sometimes said *Remember when*....
In the end, truth vanished too quietly.

Jan Zlotnik Schmidt

Madison, Wisconsin, May 1970 (After Kent State)

Inspired by "*Thirsty Boots*" by Eric Andersen

Take off your thirsty boots
and stay for a while   this was what
the curly haired lover sang to her on a dusty mile
on a day when there were fires sirens

clouds of tear gas stinging their eyes.
On a day when in a tear gas rage and haze
they were armed with stones in their pockets
ready to fling rocks at the cops.

He saw her in the midst of
rebel yells and screams.
Pigs! Pigs! After gunshots
and fallen bodies
after napalm rain fell in places so far
away they couldn't fully imagine the burning
the scorched leaves in tropical forests
or the darkness in country.

Wearily they held on to each other and stayed
for a while. He with his stout build
and wide arms that took in
her still young and muddy soul
yearning for a resting place.
Her blue velvet riding skirt flared in the sun
stuck to her skin in early morning.
Her open grin replaced by aching need.

On a dusty stretch of country road
they shared secrets   the pale yellow
green of the Plains stretching out before them.
They told each other stories and watched the sun set
stones still weighing down their pockets.
Her hair in pigtails, her denim overalls collapsing
over her thin body, she looked for the evening, the morning in his eyes.

Then later in the midst of dust and acrid smoke
he gave her a damp handkerchief to cover her mouth
her nose so she wouldn't breathe in fumes of gas
after nights with sirens blaring and searchlights
that framed the bedroom window
after they rested in the curves and warmth of their bodies
with their bloodied words and muddy selves
as the world reeled around them he was gone.

Without a word. Gone.

Now the song returns
The girl in pigtails and cowboy boots
is long gone and white stones
gathered at the edge of the shore
travel to grave sites and rest
with shards of mussels oysters clams
iridescent fragments in a bowl by her bed
The girl treks through paths of memory
through a dusty mile
through present worlds littered
with shattered glass fallen bodies fires
sirens and tears.   She wanders through
the broken places in this world
searching for the shadow of herself in the ruins.
Looking at the evening the mourning in her eyes.

ACKNOWLEDGEMENTS:

The poem, "Cease Fire," won the 2017 Raynes Poetry Competition sponsored by *Jewish Currents Magazine.* It was published in the anthology, "Borders and Boundaries" (Blue Threads Press, May, 2018).

The poem, "Portrait of a Gazan Stargazer" won Honorable Mention in the 87th Annual Poetry Competition (Non-Rhyming) sponsored by Writer's Digest (titled "Portrait of A Gazan As A Young Man").

The poem, "The Sounds of Truth Vanishing," was shortlisted for the 2018 Fish Publishing Prize. This piece was also published as part of a larger poem series, "Reverberations," by *Junto Magazine* in December, 2018.

The poem, "Kindness," was first published on May 21, 2018 by *The New Verse News.* This poem was nominated for a 2019 Pushcart Press Prize.

The poem, "The Mathematics of Parking," was first published on June 16, 2017 on the blog site **womenatwoodstock.com**

The poems, "I Am a Dutiful Daughter" and "Punta Mujeres," were published in *The Write Place at the Write Time,* and "Vermeer's Lady Writing" will be published in the 10th anniversary issue of the online journal.

The poems, "Bess's Lament" and "Madison, Wisconsin, May 1970," were published in *Chantwood Magazine, Summer 2017, Issue 9. Online.*

The poem, "Cross at the Beach," was published in *Memoir (and)* as well as in the poetry chapbook, *Hieroglyphics of Father-Daughter Time* (Word Temple Press).

The poem, "Fade Out/Fade In," was first published by *The Vassar Review* (2017).

The story, "I Met My Mother's Body at Loehmann's," was first published by *bioStories, Featured Story, July 7, 2016. Online.*

The story, *The Beer House,* won first place in the Hudson Valley Writers Guild 2013 short story contest.

AUTHORS' BIOGRAPHIES:

COLLEEN GERAGHTY: A professional social worker, Colleen is also a musician and an artist. She is a certified Amherst Writer and Artists facilitator and founder of *The Story Cottage,* a creative space for women writers and artists. Colleen's stories have appeared in *Wallkill Valley Writers Anthology 2012* and *2013* and in *A Slant of Light: Contemporary Women Writers of the Hudson Valley.* Her story, "The Beer House," received first prize in the Hudson Valley Writers Guild 2013 Short Story Contest. Two original songs from Colleen's *Deep Ravines* CD, "Hymn for Matthew" and "Nikolay," have been used to raise awareness about hate crimes and PTSD. Colleen is a member of Wallkill Valley Writers and a writing facilitator at Women of Woodstock Writing Retreat.

KIT GOLDPAUGH: Kit taught writing for over thirty years in the Hudson Valley to students ranging in age from middle school to college. Over that time, she participated in the Bard Institute for Thinking and Writing program, the Hudson Valley Writers Workshop and was awarded both a FIPSI summer grant on composition and an NEH fellowship on Women and Fiction. She lives in the People's Republic of Rosendale with her husband where they raised four sons.

EILEEN HOWARD: Eileen grew up in an Oklahoma university town, one of four siblings, all of whom spent their childhoods camping every summer with their parents. She went to Scripps College in Claremont, California and had a daughter in Hawaii and a son in Halifax, Nova Scotia before landing in New England where she went back to school to become a psychiatric nurse. Eileen worked in both hospital settings and in home care before her retirement. Eileen is an active writer and photographer and has done readings at local Hudson Valley events.

TANA MILLER: During a thirty-year career as a teacher, Tana authored language curriculum guides for her school district, co-founded and facilitated a grade 5-8 annual literary magazine, presented Whole Language workshops in Hudson Valley public schools and at the New York State Reading Conference, for which she received a commendation from the local literacy foundation. Tana co-founded and participated for ten years as a volunteer in a book group at Danbury Federal Prison for Women in Danbury, Connecticut. Tana's work has been published in several feminist journals, and in *Slant of Light* (Codhill Press). Tana was a selected reader at the Newark Public Library and has been a featured reader at local gatherings, libraries and book stores,

MARY K O'MELVENY: A retired labor rights lawyer living in Washington, DC and Woodstock, NY, Mary's poetry has appeared in print and online journals such as *GFT Press, FLARE: The Flagler Review, The Offbeat, Slippery Elm Literary Journal, Into the Void, West Texas Review* and *The Write Place at the Write Time,* as well as on various blog sites such as Women at Woodstock and "Writing in a Woman's Voice" and "The New Verse News." Mary's poetry has won several awards and honors. Her poem, "Cease Fire," won the 2017 Raynes Poetry Competition. Her poetry chapbook, "A Woman of a Certain Age," was published by Finishing Line Press in September, 2018.

JAN ZLOTNIK SCHMIDT: A SUNY Distinguished Professor of English at SUNY New Paltz, Jan's work has been published in many journals including *Kansas Quarterly, The Alaska Quarterly Review, Memoir(and),* and *The Broadkill Review.* Her work has been nominated for the Pushcart Press Prize Series. She has had two volumes of poetry published by the Edwin Mellen Press (*We Speak in Tongues,* 1991; *She had this memory,* 2000). Her chapbook, *The Earth Was Still,* was published by Finishing Line Press, and another, *Hieroglyphs of Father-Daughter Time,* was published by Word Temple Press. Most recently she co-edited with Laurence Carr a collection of works by Hudson Valley women writers entitled *A Slant of Light: Contemporary Women Writers of the Hudson Valley,* published by Codhill Press (2013).

KAPPA ADAIR WAUGH: Born into a family in which everyone – grandparents, parents, siblings – wrote, Kappa grew up assuming that writing was something all people did. She sent off a manuscript to Harcourt Brace when she was 11. Rejected. Kappa's poetry was published in school and college literary journals and, during her twenties, in *BlackRock.* More recently, Kappa's work has appeared in three editions of *Legacies,* in a poetry anthology and in *A Slant of Light.* Her work has also appeared on the poetry blog, "Writing in a Woman's Voice." A house cartoonist, Kappa recently retired after 20 happy years as Reference Librarian at Vassar College.